BOOMERANG

Andrew Garve is the pseudonym of Paul Winterton. He was born in Leicester in 1908 and after gaining an Economics degree at London University spent a year in the Soviet Union on a travelling scholarship. Returning in 1929, he joined the staff of the *Economist* and in 1933 became a reporter and later chief leader writer on the *News Chronicle*. During the latter part of the war, he was the *News Chronicle*'s Moscow correspondent and a regular broadcaster for the BBC Overseas Service. In 1947 he retired from journalism to become a full-time thriller-writer. As Andrew Garve, he has written twenty-seven stories, of which *The Megstone Plot* was filmed as *A Touch of Larceny* with James Mason and Vera Miles. Paul Winterton also writes under the pseudonyms of Roger Bax and Paul Somers.

By the same author in Pan Books

THE FAR SANDS

THE HOUSE OF SOLDIERS

THE ASHES OF LODA

FRAME-UP

CONDITIONS OF SALE

This book shall not, by way of trade or otherwise, be lent, re-sold, hired out or otherwise circulated without the publisher's prior consent in any form of binding or cover other than that in which it is published and without a similar condition including this condition being imposed on the subsequent purchaser. The book is published at a net price, and is supplied subject to the Publishers Association Standard Conditions of Sale registered under the Restrictive Trade Practices Act, 1956.

BOOMERANG

ANDREW GARVE

UNABRIDGED

PAN BOOKS LTD : LONDON

First published 1969 by Wm Collins Sons & Co Ltd.
This edition published 1972 by Pan Books Ltd,
33 Tothill Street, London, SW1.

ISBN 0 330 23362 9

© Andrew Garve 1969

Printed and bound in England by
Hazell Watson & Viney Ltd,
Aylesbury, Bucks

AUTHOR'S NOTE

Some of the roads described in this book as all-weather routes are in fact still only dry-weather routes. I hope I will be forgiven for ante-dating, in the interests of the story, the inevitable march of Australian progress.

CHAPTER I

THE OFFICES of the Commonwealth Loan Corporation in Copthall Court, London, EC were as plush as the growth of the organization had been rapid. There was a smart and courteous commissionaire to direct visitors in the foyer. There was a lift of the latest design to take them swiftly and smoothly to their destination. Glass doors opened electronically at their approach. Beyond the doors the offices were spacious, the floors close-carpeted in a delicate shade of pink, the furniture modern and elegant, the windows double-glazed against traffic noise, the air conditioned and slightly scented. A discerning depositor might well have been shocked to see how much of his money had been spent on costly overheads – but those who called at Copthall Court were not discerning and were never shocked. On the contrary, they were delighted. Opulence bred confidence.

In the outer office, the door of which said COMMONWEALTH LOAN CORPORATION. INQUIRIES, there was an efficient, highly paid and extremely decorative secretary, and two mini-skirted copy typists. Behind one of the inner doors, inscribed JAMES FURNEVAL, SECRETARY, there sat a middle-aged Scotsman of unimpeachable integrity who, with the help of two male assistants, took care of all the clerical work including the records of deposits and withdrawals. He was devoted to his job, his company, and his Chief – but he was never called upon to make executive decisions. Behind the other inner door, not inscribed at all, was the dynamo and brain of the organization, the chairman, the managing director and for all practical purposes the sole boss, Peter Talbot. He occupied an expensive leather chair behind an expensive rosewood desk, and was flanked by every conceivable office gadget and device including a cocktail cabinet with drinks and cigars for the entertainment of important visitors.

Talbot was thirty-three years old. He was good-looking, taller than average, lean about the face and slim in build. His eyes were alert, his movements decisive, his manner assured. He was meticulously groomed and impeccably dressed. He had style and distinction.

Talbot had personally created the Commonwealth Loan Corporation, and in five years had built it up from a name in the telephone directory to a powerful financial organization with wide-ranging interests. He had done so by paying his depositors at least one per cent more than anyone else would have done, and lending their money at an extremely profitable margin for various productive if somewhat speculative enterprises. The turnover had grown rapidly and was now huge. There had been moments of unusual liquidity when he could have signed a Corporation cheque for a million pounds and had it honoured without question. There had been several occasions, in the course of his active and often daring investment transactions, when he had called his broker – Harry Prendergast, of Lewis, Arbuthnot and Lane – and bought a quarter of a million pounds' worth of shares for his private account on the simple credit of his name. His meteoric rise had been watched by his City colleagues with respect and envy. Here, it seemed, was a man of sound judgement as well as flair, a man whose enterprises always prospered and whose stock-market dealings always paid off. A City prodigy, a financial whizz-kid, well on his way to multi-millionairedom and tycoonery.

Talbot himself was less sure about that. He was a gambler whose luck had held for nearly five years, but he knew he could as easily finish up a loser as a winner, which of course was what made gambling so fascinating. The road to wealth and power had as many pitfalls as the moon had craters and only recently he'd stumbled into a quite sizeable one – fortunately without publicity. He was having a worrying time, and his problems were not the kind he could share.

At five o'clock that evening – a Friday in June that he was never afterwards to forget – he collected his Aston Martin convertible from the underground garage below the office and drove to Kensington, where his girlfriend of the moment had a flat. She was a film starlet named Serena whom he'd met six months before when the Corporation had been financing a modest production. Their affair hadn't been exactly a grand passion, but it had temporarily satisfied them both. Serena had enjoyed the clothes and jewellery that Talbot had given her. Talbot had enjoyed Serena, who was blonde, shapely, sexy, and extremely pretty. As a playmate she was as good as they came, and in a superficial way he'd become quite attached to her. He was looking forward now to a playful evening which would soothe his cares away.

As soon as she opened the door, he knew he was in for a disappointment. She was dressed for an evening out, not for an evening in. She gave him a perfunctory kiss, and said, 'Let's drive to that place by the river at Maidenhead, darling. I feel like some fresh air.'

Talbot's face took on the sulky look of the deprived male. 'Bit of a drag, isn't it? I was rather hoping for a spot of domesticity.'

'Oh, don't be stuffy. Anyway, I've booked a table.'

Fuming inwardly, he followed her out to the car. The rush hour traffic was still at its height. There'd be precious little fresh air on the road to Maidenhead, he thought. Especially at a weekend. However, once they were on their way, his mood improved. He enjoyed driving, especially in a fast open car, and the Aston Martin was a beauty. By the time they'd reached the waterside roadhouse, he had almost recovered his good humour.

They had a couple of martinis, and settled down to a long, leisurely, gourmet meal, matched by a bottle of excellent claret. Talbot was fastidious about food and drink, as he was about most material things, and good wine was his second greatest pleasure. Gradually, he forgot his cares. Serena was in sparkling form, and had never looked prettier. Dancing with her after dinner wasn't quite as enjoyable as going to bed with her, but he found it no hardship.

It was around eleven o'clock, when at Serena's suggestion they were splitting a bottle of Bollinger, that she suddenly said, 'I've got news for you, darling.'

He looked at her sharply. 'Oh?'

'I'm going to Italy. I've got a part in a film that Scarlatti's going to make, called *Never Say Die*. It's not a big part, but it's right up my street, and the film's going to be a top feature, with Emilio Grandi and Victoria Guest, so it may be the start of really big things for me ...' She pouted prettily. 'Well, aren't you going to congratulate me?'

'Of course,' Talbot said. 'Congratulations! When are you going?'

'Tomorrow. I'm flying with Scarlatti at eleven.'

'How long do you expect to be away?'

'Only about six months, unless I go on to Hollywood afterwards. We'll be on location in Sicily a lot of the time – isn't it exciting? And Scarlatti's a wonderful director – in fact he's a wonderful person, beside being fabulously rich. I think he's taken quite a fancy to me ... Peter, why are you looking so glum? You want me to get on, don't you?'

'I'll miss you,' Talbot said.

'Well, of course you will, silly, and I'll miss you, too – but it *is* my big chance. Anyway, it's been wonderful knowing you – I'll never forget the lovely times we've had together. And I will write as soon as I get a free moment, and tell you everything that happens.'

'That'll be nice!' Talbot said – and beckoned the waiter to bring his bill.

Serena was unaware of any crisis. She sat back in her seat,

her mink coat wrapped around her, relaxed and pleasantly sleepy. She had enjoyed her last evening with darling Peter – and tomorrow she would be flying off with Scarlatti. What heaven life was!

Talbot drove in angry discomfort, the champagne sour in his stomach. A filthy drink, champagne – all gas and acid. What a lousy day it had been, from first to last. Worry at the office, frustration in the evening – and now this unfeeling walk-out. Damn it, she could at least have given him a bit of warning. Not just sprung it on him at the last moment. There were decencies to be observed, even between transients.

It wasn't that he had any deep affection for her. Not *deep*. He'd realized long ago that she was empty-headed and selfish and predatory. The affair would probably have fizzled out pretty soon anyway. And he certainly wasn't making any moral judgements. Whatever else he was, he wasn't a hypocrite. They'd both been amusing themselves – nothing more. They'd both known that. If she wanted to make a play for the Scarlatti fellow, she had a perfect right to. All the same, it irked him that it was she who'd made the break, not he. He wasn't used to that. It was bruising to the ego – humiliating. And he *would* miss her. Stupid, but true. That bloody wop and his stinking pictures...

He drove faster on the way back, shifting his gears savagely, ramming his foot down, relieving his feelings by speed and noise. He half hoped that Serena would react, would even show fear at his recklessness. He would get a kick out of that. Not that there was any danger. It was nearly one in the morning and the traffic was thin. Anyway, Serena was almost asleep. To hell with her! To hell with everything...!

He was still driving fast as he entered the built-up suburbs of west London. He wasn't aware just how fast till he heard a warning bell behind him. His eyes flicked to the speedometer. The needle showed sixty-five. He looked in the mirror. A black police car was closing up quickly. Serena came, to life, and glanced back, and clutched his arm.

For a second he slowed. Then his pent-up irritation exploded in action. God! – hadn't he been pushed around enough for one day? 'Fasten your seat belt!' he shouted. 'I'm going to lose them.' He pressed his foot to the boards and the Aston surged forward.

He was committed now. It was his skill against theirs. He braked and turned, roaring through unfamiliar streets, poised to swerve or slow at crossings where the lights showed red, opening to full throttle in the straight stretches, exhilarated by the whistling wind and the wild horses under the bonnet. He was driving well – he knew he was driving well. But the police car was gaining on him, closing the gap with shrieking tyres. Second by second the sound of its bell grew louder. It was almost on his tail. No good! – he'd never make it. Better give up, before he broke his neck. He braked hard, turned for the kerb, mounted it – and came to rest in a shower of glass with the bonnet of the car poking through a shattered shop window.

'You fool!' Serena said.

The police approached him cautiously, as though they half expected to find a violent criminal at the wheel. There were four of them. One was a sergeant, who paused for a moment by the car, taking in the scene, grimly surveying the mess. Then he said, with dangerous calm, 'May I see your licence, sir?'

Talbot reached for the glove pocket, fumbling at the catch, groping inside. He knew the licence was there – he always kept it in exactly the same place. Damned elusive tonight, though... Ah, now he'd got it. He handed it over. It was a clean licence. In fifteen years of driving, he'd never so much as had an incident.

The sergeant glanced at it. 'Have you been drinking, sir?'

'Of course I've been drinking,' Talbot said. His tone suggested that no sensible man would do anything else. 'But I'm reasonably sober.'

'We'll see, sir. I must ask you to take a breath test.' A constable went back to the police car and returned with a little bag. Talbot blew into it, not without difficulty. He saw for himself that the reading was higher than the law allowed. A lot higher.

'Right,' said the sergeant. 'You'd better come along to the station – both of you. We'll see to your car.'

It was just two weeks later that Talbot came before the magistrates at West London Police Court. In those two weeks he had had several planning sessions with Furneval, and as far as possible he had left the Corporation's affairs in order. He had taken no steps in his defence. Having been apprised of the charges against him, he had decided there was no point in wasting his own or anyone else's time in trying to answer them. Driving to the public danger, driving at eighty-seven miles per hour in a built-up area, driving with a blood-alcohol content exceeding the legal limit, failing to stop when required by the police, crossing three sets of traffic lights when at red, causing damage to property through reckless driving. All true ... Well, he'd always reckoned himself a good loser.

He'd been an idiot, of course. A lunatic. Driving in that state. And making a dash for it instead of stopping. He knew now that he'd been very far from sober. Otherwise he'd never have given way to such a crazy impulse. He'd certainly asked for it. And he was going to get it ...

He glanced around the court. Back in the public seats, he recognized the faithful Furneval. He managed a twisted smile. Furneval smiled back, encouragingly. A dim man, Furneval – but loyal ... No Serena, naturally. She was probably in bed with Scarlatti. She'd always preferred the mornings ...

The magistrate peered down from his dais. 'Peter Edward

Talbot, you have pleaded guilty to all the charges preferred against you. Have you anything to say?'

Talbot gave a slight shrug. 'Only that I'd had a – a bit of a quarrel with my girlfriend, sir. I was feeling rather upset. But I realize that's no excuse.'

'No,' said the magistrate, 'it isn't. You might easily have killed someone. Your conduct was irresponsible and reckless. In the circumstances, I should be failing in my duty if I showed any leniency. You will pay a fine of £100 and go to prison for ninety days, and you will be disqualified from driving a motor vehicle for two years. Next case.'

Talbot loathed Wormwood Scrubs. It wasn't so much the feeling of being confined by walls that troubled him – after all, with full remission he'd only be there for two months, which wasn't long enough to bring on serious claustrophobia. What he found intolerable was the smell, the noise, the almost uneatable food, and having to sleep three in a cell with uncongenial companions. It was a humiliating price to pay for a few minutes' crazy behaviour. From the start, his sights were firmly fixed on the date of his release.

He had no complaints about his personal treatment. On the contrary, several special privileges had been extended to him which he appreciated – like being allowed to use the library at will, to have the financial papers sent in to him, and up to a point to pursue his business. He was twice visited by Furneval – who on the second occasion brought disturbing news about the Corporation.

'I'm afraid,' the secretary said, 'that the rate of new deposits has fallen off quite substantially, Mr Talbot. By about thirty per cent in the eight weeks since your – er – accident. And withdrawals have increased by roughly the same percentage.'

Talbot grunted. This, from the moment he'd sobered up, was what he'd foreseen and feared. It was illogical that depositors should fight shy of a perfectly sound finance company just because its chairman had been jailed for a couple of months for a motoring offence, but that was how their minds had worked. In this line of business, confidence was everything, and it was indivisible.

'How's the trend now?' he asked.

'It's improving slowly, sir – I hope the worst is over. But of course our reserves have taken a knock. And I gather there's a bit of gossip going on about us in the City.'

'Gossip about what?'

'Well, I've heard nothing specific ... I imagine it's to do with our solvency.'

'Ridiculous,' Talbot said. 'Still, these rumours can do a lot of damage – we'll have to scotch them. You'd better put out a statement. Say the Corporation has ample reserves to meet all contingencies, and that its profit for the current year will be well up to expectations.'

Furneval hesitated. 'You'll recall, sir, that Oil Exploration are behind with their interest payments, and may be in quite serious trouble. We could drop a packet there.'

'If we do, Furneval, we'll more than make it up in some other direction. I've got several promising plans for the immediate future, and I'll take full responsibility for the statement.'

Furneval looked relieved. 'Very well, Mr Talbot, I'll get something out today ... And may I say how much we're all looking forward to seeing you back in the office.'

'Thank you,' Talbot said. 'I share your feeling.'

As he lay in his cell that night, with a pillow around his ears to mute the snores of a neighbour, Talbot realistically reviewed the Corporation's affairs and his own in the light of Furneval's report – and his conclusion was that he was in deep trouble.

Not just ordinary City trouble. Not the mere danger of failure, bankruptcy and liquidation, which could happen to anyone. Much worse than that. He knew, as no one else knew, that his long-term freedom was at risk.

The fact was that shortly after the last audit, he had juggled some £125,000 of the Corporation's funds into his private account. He had done it partly to meet the expenses of his very high standard of living – to say nothing of Serena's – but largely to finance a promising investment in a South African gold mine. For once, Lady Luck had been against him. A week after his purchase the mine had been flooded by an inrush of underground water, and the shares had halved in value almost overnight. On the best available technical advice he'd sold near the bottom, fearing a total loss, and had then had the mortification of seeing the shares steadily creep up again as the news had improved. The disastrous venture had left him with liquid assets of a few thousand pounds in various banks, some twenty thousand pounds' worth of US dollar bills cached in a safe at home as an insurance against the worst contingency – and a net shortfall of some £100,000.

In the normal course of events, with funds flowing smoothly into the Corporation, business booming, investment income rising and profits leaping, he'd have hoped to make up a substantial part of his losses out of his annual 'cut', use the money for quick and fruitful speculation, and juggle the £125,000 back before the next audit. But now, with the run on deposits that had followed his jail sentence, the inevitable restriction of new business, and the coming Oil Exploration fiasco, he knew he hadn't a chance.

That being so, the outlook was starkly plain. With reasonable good fortune and a bit of bluff the situation could be held until the auditors got to work again in January, still six months away. Then the deficit would be uncovered – and within weeks, if he were still around, he'd be back in Wormwood Scrubs. Not just for ninety days, either. The courts were merciless with fraudulent converters, betrayers of trust, especially when the savings of the little man were involved.

He'd get seven years – and he'd have to serve five of them. Five years in this stinking hole! It was unthinkable.

There was only one way out – short of abandoning everything he'd worked for. Somehow he'd got to lay his hands on £100,000 in the next six months. It wasn't, by his standards, such a large sum. At least twice in the past, when things had been going well, he'd had three or four times that amount in his private accounts. But that had been when his stock market gambles had been coming off – and gambles had a way of coming off best when nothing much hung on them. Also, he'd had the money to risk. To try for a big coup now, with no resources behind him, would be to invite a quick disaster. So what else was there? Credit? An overdraft? Not much chance of that, while the current squeeze was on – certainly not for any useful period. Besides, he'd hardly dare to ask for a large credit now, in case someone suggested looking at the Corporation's books. It wasn't as though he had any collateral to speak of – his shares in the Corporation were already mortgaged to the hilt. A personal loan from a friend? For £100,000 without security? He must be joking ...

All the same, he'd got to raise that money somehow. He'd *got* to.

He continued to mull over his problem by day and by night. Seeking a way. An honest way or a devious one – it didn't matter which, as long as it came off. He was desperate enough for a bank raid or a jewel grab – though that sort of thing usually involved violence against persons, for which he had no taste at all. It would also require expert associates, which he lacked. Anyway, it wasn't the kind of enterprise he could put his heart into. He was a man of ingenuity and resource, not crude physical action. A planner rather than a doer. There was only one way he could hope to retrieve the position, a way he knew and understood – by using his wits. But where, and how?

He was still thinking about it when, a week before he was due to be released, he was moved to a new cell.

2

He waited with some anxiety to see who would be occupying the other two beds in the cell. He'd met some fairly unpleasant characters in Wormwood Scrubs, and he'd no desire to spend his remaining seven days in the company of a strangler or a dope pusher. One had one's standards.

He wasn't kept long in suspense. In a few minutes the door clanged back and another prisoner was brought in. Talbot couldn't remember having seen him before. He was a stocky man of about forty, very powerfully built, with a craggy, weather-worn face the colour of old leather. The warder indicated the bed he was to occupy, and left without speaking. The man peeled off his jacket, sat down on the bed, and rolled up his shirt sleeves, displaying forearms almost as thick as Talbot's thighs.

Talbot eyed him warily. 'Hallo,' he said.

The man nodded. 'How y'goin'?'

'My name's Talbot. Peter Talbot.'

'Frank Dawes,' said the newcomer. His tone was friendly, his accent an offbeat Cockney twang. 'What are you in for, sport?'

'Motoring offences,' Talbot said.

'Bad luck! What did they give you?'

'Ninety days – but I've only seven more to do.'

'Good on us both, then. I'm out next week, too.'

'You're Australian, are you?'

'Born and raised in New South Wales. Finest State in the finest country.' Dawes began stowing his few belongings in the receptacles provided.

'What are *you* in for?' Talbot asked.

'I dropped a cop outside a pub,' Dawes said.

'Dropped a cop . . . ?' For a moment, Talbot was puzzled. 'Do you mean you hit him?'

'Too right, I did. Knocked him cold . . . They gave me four months for it.'

'Four months! That was a bit steep, wasn't it?'

'Well, I busted his nose.'

'Ah . . .' Talbot thoughtfully studied his companion. He seemed an amiable enough man, at least at the moment. 'What's your line of country?' he asked.

'Work, you mean?'

'Yes.'

'Mining.'

'Any special job?'

'Just pretty well everything. Driller, shot firer, loader, gang foreman, mechanic, engineer – I've done the lot.'

'All in Australia?'

'I had a couple of years in the States – but mostly Australia. The Kal, the Boulder, the Lyall, the Hill – you name a mining town, I've worked there. Last place was the Henry. I don't suppose you've heard of the Henry.'

'Would that be Mount Henry Proprietary?'

'That's the one. Up in Queensland, south of the Gulf. About eighty miles north of the Isa.'

Talbot nodded. 'It mines copper and silver, doesn't it?'

'And lead and zinc. It's a bonza mine – about the richest there is in its line, after the Isa . . . How come you know about it?'

'The company's registered in London and its shares are quoted here. I'm interested in companies . . . I work in the City.'

'That so . . . ?' There was a little silence. 'I can't stand cities – they give me a pain in the guts. I go for small places like the Henry – three or four thousand people, everything you want laid on by the company, and empty country all round.'

'It's isolated, is it?'

'I'll say. It's twenty miles from the nearest settlement. Place called Linda – that's the railhead. And Linda's only a dump.'

'M'm . . . It must be quite a problem getting stuff in and out.'

Dawes shook his head. 'No problem at all. The company built a fine bitumen road up through the hills – decided it was cheaper than a rail spur. Everything goes up and down in trucks and containers. It's an all-weather road – the traffic keeps moving even in the wet. Most of the time, anyway.'

'You get a lot of rain up there, do you?'

'Too right, we do! I've known fifteen inches fall in twenty-four hours when the monsoon gets going. The whole countryside's flooded then – you can't move off the bitumen. But it's dry for about nine months of the year – and when it's dry, the climate's a beaut.'

'Why did you leave?' Talbot asked.

Dawes gave a rather sheepish grin. 'I dropped a cop there, too.'

'No! Really?'

'My word, yes. A sergeant. He tried to pinch a sheila I was going around with.'

'Then I don't blame you,' Talbot said, thinking of Scarlatti. 'All the same, it's a dangerous habit – cop-bashing.'

'You're telling me! But I hate cops – there's something about them that makes me do my block. Specially when I've got a drop of grog inside me . . . Anyway, they shoved me in the cooler for thirty days. When I came out I thought I'd like a change of scene, so I cashed my savings and came to England for a look-see. First time over.'

'What do you think of it?'

'Well, no offence, sport, but I reckon it's a run-down old country. Full of blacks and Commies and spongers. All this welfare – it's like a bloody soup kitchen. No enterprise, no spirit.'

Talbot smiled. 'You won't be staying, then?'

'Not me! Right now I've done my money, but as soon as I can raise the fare I'll be getting back to the sun and the open spaces.'

'Back to mining, too?'

'I dunno . . . What I'd like would be to make a big chunk of dough, live it up, travel around the world. I've got itchy feet. I guess it's not that easy, though.'

'No,' Talbot agreed. 'It's not easy at all . . .'

They broke off as the cell door opened again and another man was brought in. Talbot and Dawes both recognized him at once – and with pleasure, for he was the most popular man in the jail. At a prison concert a couple of weeks before, he'd imitated the chaplain with such perfect mimicry that even the Assistant Governor had been primly amused. He was a man of about Talbot's age, with a plump, rubbery face, twinkling blue eyes and a big Roman nose.

'Hi, fellows,' he said cheerfully. 'Mind if I doss down with you?'

'Glad to have you,' Talbot said. 'This is Frank Dawes. He's a cop-basher. My name's Talbot. I drive too fast.'

The new man nodded. 'I'm Desmond Holt.'

'We saw you at the sing-song,' Dawes said. 'That was a bonza act you did – real great . . . What are you in for, sport?'

'A little matter of ten thousand cigars,' Holt told him. 'Someone forgot to declare them.'

'Smuggler, eh?'

'Only an amateur so far.'

'How did you get into the racket?'

Holt shrugged. 'You could say I drifted into it. I was a radio officer in the Green Cross Line till the company shut down its passenger services. Then I was stuck for a job. I joined up with a couple of old shipmates who reckoned they could make a packet smuggling tobacco in with the freight. I still think they'd got something – but we slipped up. We were rumbled the very first time.'

'No kidding,' Dawes said. 'What did it cost you?'

'A heck of a fine, and thirty days. But I've only four more to do, praise the lord.'

'Then what?'

Holt's mouth pursed – and by what seemed to Talbot a miracle of virtuosity, the thin, cultured voice of the Assistant Governor emerged from it. 'Well, goodbye, Holt, and good luck. I trust we shan't see you here again.' Then Holt, *au naturel* – 'No, sir, I intend to be more careful next time.'

Dawes gave a loud guffaw. Talbot smiled.

The evening passed agreeably, at times even hilariously. Holt, with a fresh audience to appreciate his talents, was in top form. Talbot and Dawes both had interesting shop talk to contribute. For hours the three men chatted, swapping stories and experiences and attitudes, opening out to each other in a way they'd hardly have done outside prison. The talk was so stimulating and the company so congenial that for a while Talbot was even able to forget his gnawing private anxiety.

It was Dawes who said at last, 'Well, pals, how about a spot of kip? I reckon this galah session's gone on long enough.'

'This *what*?' Talbot said.

'Galah session.' Dawes accented the second syllable. 'G-A-L-A-H. You never heard the expression?'

Talbot shook his head.

'But you've heard of our Flying Doctor Service down under?'

'Vaguely, yes. I can't say I know a lot about it.'

'You should, it's famous – there's nothing like it in the world. Covers two-thirds of Australia now. Want to hear?'

'Of course – go ahead.'

'Well, it was started about forty years ago by a cove named Flynn. "Flynn of the Inland." He got the idea of setting up a chain of radio bases and giving two-way transceivers to folk who were stuck out on their own, so they could keep in touch with civilization. Mostly people living on stations in the outback and blokes travelling alone in the Never Never. Just so if they got crook or ran into any trouble, they could call up their Base for help.' Dawes looked at Holt. 'You must know about it, sport.'

Holt nodded. 'Sure – but it's up my street.'

'Go on,' Talbot said. 'Where does the galah come in?'

'I'm telling you. Every day there are two regular sessions on the air – that's when people who want advice from the doctor, or want to send telegrams or urgent messages, call up Base from the outposts. Then, when the serious business is over, all the housewives for hundreds of miles around get down to a good old gossip on the radio. Everyone listens and anyone can join in. I heard them at it once, on a set at the Henry. Boy, did they jabber! And that's what we call the galah session.'

'But why galah?' Talbot asked.

'The galah's an Aussie parrot,' Dawes said. 'Never stops talking.'

There was no special or single aspect of his encounter with Dawes and Holt that started Talbot on his train of thought next day. He was not even aware of thought as his agile mind ranged over a mass of material, sifting and testing and rejecting. The process was unconscious. He was simply working on the available ingredients, like yeast on dough ... The fact that the two men were due to be released about the same time that he was. Their obvious readiness to make money without too much scruple. Holt's radio knowledge and histrionic gifts. The Australian background of Dawes, his mining expertise, his familiarity with a terrain that had exciting possibilities. The interesting details that had emerged about the galah session. And Talbot himself, with his City know-how, his still unquestioned financial standing, his wide contacts, his temporary access to other people's cash. These were the seeds on the fertile ground of Talbot's imagination as he sat in the prison library that morning, making out catalogue cards. And that morning the seeds began to germinate.

He would need, of course, a lot more information. He would need to probe and explore, to ask Dawes many questions. A single unfavourable answer might be enough to kill the embryo idea stone dead. In all probability that was what would happen. Still, it seemed worth a try.

He debated how to proceed. There were obvious dangers in disclosing what was in his mind to new and untried companions. He'd have preferred to make his first approaches cautiously, to take a few more soundings before rushing in. But in the circumstances that was hardly possible. It would be no good pretending he was asking his questions out of simple curiosity – they'd be too detailed and too bizarre for that. Dawes would realize at once there was something in the wind, and he'd want to know what. Anyone would. So it looked, Talbot thought, as though he'd have to take a chance and come clean right away. Or partly clean . . .

He introduced the subject in a casual tone, shortly after the three men had been returned to their cell after supper.

'When I was working in the library today, fellows,' he said, 'I had what I thought was a rather promising idea . . . I don't know whether either of you would be interested, but if you were it might do us all a bit of good.'

Holt shot him a quick glance. 'Legal?'

'Not particularly.'

'Then hold it.' Holt started to move around the cell, inspecting the light fixture high up on the ceiling, the walls. In the end he appeared satisfied. 'I was wondering if the place was bugged,' he said. 'But I don't suppose it is. Not really British, bugging a cell! Anyway, I can't see anything. Go ahead.'

Talbot turned to Dawes. 'It's about that mine of yours. Mount Henry. Would you mind if I asked you a few questions? I'll explain why later.'

Dawes looked a bit surprised. But he said, 'Ask anything you like, sport.'

'Good. First of all, then – those transceivers you were talking about last night. You did say there was one at the mine, didn't you?'

'That's right.'

'Is it used much?'

'Only when the phone goes crook,' Dawes said, 'and that's not often. Maybe once every two or three years, after a specially bad storm. It was put in when the company first started up, before the telephone lines were carried through. Now it's just kept for emergencies.'

'Are there any other sets in the town?'

'Not two-way ones. There used to be a few to start with, before the phone was connected, but they were all called in.'

'Are you sure of that?'

'You bet I'm sure. Those sets are only licensed for folk who don't have any other way to communicate. People in the back-blocks, and travellers – like I told you. If everyone was allowed to have them, the air would be full of gabble all the time.'

'Yes, I see . . . Do you happen to know where the mine's set is kept?'

'Last I heard of it, it was in a school.'

'A *school*? Why?'

'They used it there right at the beginning, before there were any proper teachers. There's a radio programme goes out called *School of the Air*, and that was all the kids had to start with . . . Afterwards I guess no one bothered to take the set away.'

'Aha . . . What's the school like? A brick building?'

'No, it's a wooden bungalow, built up high, with a verandah. Pretty much like an ordinary house.'

'Does anyone live there? A caretaker?'

'No . . . Who'd want to live in a school?'

'So it's empty at night?'

'Sure.'

There was a short pause as Talbot mentally assembled his next series of questions. Then he said, 'Does the town have an airstrip?'

Dawes shook his head. 'There's no place flat enough for one at the Henry – the ground's like a roller coaster. You couldn't even get a flivver down safely . . . The nearest airstrip's at the bottom of the bitumen at Linda – alongside the railway. If anyone's flying in, a company car meets the plane there.'

'What about helicopters?'

'They're not used much – they're too tricky and slow, and their range is small. With a good airstrip and a bonza road, a light plane's better.'

'But a helicopter *could* land at the Henry?'

'Oh, sure.'

'In the monsoon?'

'Christ, no – not unless the pilot was tired of life. He'd get washed out of the sky.'

Talbot gave a satisfied grunt. 'Well, that all seems quite hopeful . . . Now about this bitumen road. What sort of country does it run through?'

'Pretty rugged country,' Dawes said. 'There's a sharpish rise from the plain to the tableland, with a steep edge – what we call the "jump-up". After that it's all hills and ridges with dry watercourses in between. The road winds up beside one of the watercourses. A good bit of the time it runs through a gorge.'

'Is there much traffic on the road at night?'

'At night? – no . . . The trucks only operate in daylight unless there's something special on – and there's not much private traffic after dark. Just the odd utility, maybe, coming back from the weekend trip to the Gulf. Locally, there's nowhere much worth going to. Folks'd sooner stay at the Henry and watch a movie.'

'What about the ground above the road? Do people wander about there?'

'Oh, my word, no. I tell you, it's empty. A wilderness – no error. A bloke could get crook there and not be found for a year.'

'What sort of cover does it offer? For cars, say?'

'Plenty. There are quite a few rock overhangs – and lots of low scrub. Gum and acacia.'

Talbot nodded. 'Where do the telephone wires run – alongside the road?'

'That's right. All the way.'

'You said yesterday that in the wet season the ground's impassable for wheeled traffic, apart from the road. Is that really a fact?'

'Too right, it is! When the floods are on, even a horse can't make it through the bush.'

'But you can always be sure of getting through on the road?'

'Yeah, if you take a bit of care.'

'When does the wet season start?'

'Usually late December. Middle of the summer. We reckon to get a few scattered thunderstorms first – just the odd inch or two of rain that runs off quick – and then around Christmas the downpour starts. That's when the monsoon really breaks.'

'Is it reliable?'

'It's more reliable up there than in most parts. You can pretty well count on the end of December – give or take a week or two.'

'Do you get good weather forecasts?'

'Better than most, I reckon – specially when the wet's due. It's the big news for everyone. I'd say we have a pretty fair idea what's coming.'

Talbot gave another satisfied nod. 'Tell me, who runs the mine? Who's the manager?'

'A bloke named Ivor Williams. Welsh by birth, though he comes from England.'

'What's he like?'

'Small, tough, about fifty. Knows the job inside out.'

'Who does he ring up in the company if he wants to report something?'

'Depends on the importance. There's a local office at the Isa – he talks to the company's rep there quite a bit. Cove named Gregory. If it's big stuff he calls up Melbourne on the long-distance. That's where the head office is.'

'Right. Now one more question. Is Mount Henry very closely policed?'

'No more than any other township. The Henry's not like a gold mine – no one's going to make off with a lump of copper sulphide or even a bar of silver. It's not worth risking the job for. Blokes are pretty highly paid up there.'

'Fine,' Talbot said. 'Okay – that's the lot . . . So now we come to the big question. Would you fellows be prepared to take a few chances, outside the law, for a sizeable chunk of dough?'

'How big a chunk?'

'I'll tell you that in a minute. I just want to know whether you're with me in principle.'

'I wouldn't turn anything down out of hand,' Holt said. Talbot looked at Dawes.

'Nor would I, sport,' Dawes said. 'What's on your mind?'

Thirty minutes, and an awed silence, later, Talbot came to the end of his monologue. 'Well, there you are,' he said. 'That's the gist of it.'

Holt gazed at him with unconcealed admiration. 'And to think I've been doing time for a lousy crate of cigars. Oh, boy!'

'You like the idea?'

'I'm knocked sideways . . . Mind you, I don't know whether it would work in practice – I'd need convincing. But simply as an idea, it's a honey. A stroke of genius. Maestro, I salute you.'

'What about you, Dawes?'

Dawes said slowly, 'I don't see why it shouldn't work – our end of it, anyway. I reckon it's a mighty plan – you've fitted the pieces together real good-o . . . Matter of fact, I'd get quite a kick out of it.'

'You'd get a lot more than that,' Talbot said.

'How much?' Holt asked again.

'Well, we'd aim at cleaning up three hundred thousand pounds altogether – and I think we could do it.'

Holt gave a low whistle.

'In fact I'm so sure of it that I'd settle for an equal three-way split – even though I've *got* to clear a hundred thousand myself to get out of the red and stay out of jail.'

There was a short, reflective silence. Then Dawes said, 'It'd cost a packet to set up the expedition. Where would that come from?'

'I'd find it,' Talbot said.

'How – if you're so short of dough?'

'I'm short of big dough, not chicken feed . . . Anyway, I'd draw expenses. Theoretically I'd be on the company's business. Working for my depositors. The amount wouldn't be questioned till January. By then, if the plan came off, I'd be in a position to square things up. If it didn't, I'd be sunk anyway.'

Dawes grunted.

Holt said, 'There'd be a few lively moments, of course.'

'Yes, there would. The trickiest part would be at the mine. The demolition job could be a bit of a cliffhanger, too. And getting the message over . . . But once we were past those hurdles we'd be home and dry.'

'As long as no one ever found out we'd been around there at the same time,' Holt said. 'After having been together in the same prison cell. Someone might start putting three and three together!'

Talbot nodded. 'I agree – that's most important. To be on the safe side, I think we'd have to go out by different routes, to different ports, and travel three ways to the rendezvous. With good cover stories, of course. And then always meet secretly. We could arrange that, with care.'

'There'd be the same problem after we got back,' Holt said. 'How would you pay us out without setting up a connexion between us...? In cash?'

'No – I wouldn't want to draw all that money in cash. Much too dangerous . . . But as it happens, I keep several accounts in different banks under different names. I'd pay the necessary sums in by post, probably in several instalments, and draw cheques in your favour in those names. No problem at all.'

'Couldn't the authorities work back from us to your accounts, and then, with a little sleuthing, on to you?'

Talbot shook his head. 'They wouldn't work back from you because you'd never be in the picture at all. That's the whole point. The only person who could come under suspicion would be me. And I'd have a complete answer.'

'You certainly make it sound very simple,' Holt said. 'Of course – forgive me for raising this – we would have to trust you over the cut, wouldn't we? Especially if you were going to get back here first.'

'That's so,' Talbot agreed. 'You *would* have to trust me – even though you may think I'm not exactly a gilt-edged security. There's no other way.'

Holt looked at Dawes. 'Any views on that, Aussie?'

Dawes gently massaged the bulging muscles of his right forearm. 'I think we could trust him,' he said. 'I'm pretty handy with me dooks!'

They all grinned amiably at each other.

'Well,' Talbot said, 'what's the general feeling? Do we go on with it, or not? Holt?'

'I'm for going on, Maestro. Provisionally, anyway.'

Dawes nodded. 'No harm in talking about it.'

'Right,' Talbot said. 'Then let's start getting down to details . . .'

CHAPTER II

BY THE end of November, when the southern part of Queensland was moving into its sub-tropical summer, Talbot had been in Brisbane for more than a fortnight and had almost worked through his programme of business talks. During his stay he had met the heads of several travel agencies, conferred with the manager of the leading garage chain, visited three government departments, and outlined his plans to two constructional companies. Now, on the thirtieth of the month, he was on his way to the last of his interviews – with the Director of Tourism, a man named William Harper, who had been out of town since his arrival.

As his taxi bore him over the William Jolly Bridge towards the Office of Tourism, his mood was relaxed. The arduous nature of the enterprise ahead had not prevented him from enjoying his couple of weeks in Brisbane. Rather to his surprise, he'd found it a city of much grace, with many of its older buildings pure Regency. He'd liked its hilly setting and its backcloth of high mountains to the west. He'd liked its carpet of parks and gardens with their palms and orange trees and big shady mangoes and the blazing scarlet of the poinsettias that lined the roads. He'd liked the yacht-dotted river that wound in placid reaches through the city; the verandahed Queensland houses built eight or ten feet up on stilts; the healthy, suntanned people with their leisurely, easy-going manner. And after London in November he'd particularly liked the temperature, which was just comfortable in the high seventies.

At the Tourist Office he was received by a stunning girl secretary with honey-coloured hair and a golden complexion. He eyed her – as he'd eyed so many glowing girls in

Brisbane – with detached appreciation. On this trip, women were out, asceticism was in. There must be no distractions, no deflections from the goal. He gave his name and was shown at once into the Director's room.

William Harper was a pleasant, white-haired man with the engaging drawl of the Queenslander. He greeted Talbot with a warm smile and firm handshake, expressed his regret that their meeting had been so long delayed, and got straight down to business.

'So you're interested in financing a chain of motels in Queensland,' he said, fingering the letter of introduction on his desk.

'That's right, Mr Harper. The project's still in a very early stage, of course – but if I can get it off the ground, my company, the Commonwealth Loan Corporation, would propose to put about a million into it to start with. Pounds sterling, that is, not Australian dollars. I've been having some exploratory talks these past couple of weeks with various interested people here, and I must say I've been favourably impressed by the prospects. But I'd very much like to hear your views before I go any further.'

'Well,' Harper said, 'I'm not a financier, but I'd certainly think there were great opportunities. We're a rapidly developing State with a thriving economy and a rising population, and there's no visible limit to the potential of the tourist business. We've got everything here in Queensland to attract people – sunshine practically all the time, mild winters, splendid beaches, magnificent scenery. We're getting tourists now from all over the world, not just Australia – and the season's getting longer every year ... Of course, there's been a certain amount of development already, as you've probably noticed. What part of the State have you in mind for these motels?'

'Preferably the less well-known part,' Talbot said. 'I haven't had a chance to see much of your famous coastline yet, but I'm told that between the Gold Coast and the

Barrier Reef area there are already something like five hundred motels built or building on the main highway – which sounds as though it's pretty well supplied. I was thinking rather of the interior – "out west" I believe you call it – where my Corporation could expect to get in on the ground floor. More of a pioneering effort.'

'Well, you'd certainly find very little competition out west at the moment,' Harper said. 'Our inland is still very empty country, and a lot of it isn't easily accessible. But we're spending millions of dollars on road improvements every year, and the traffic's steadily increasing.'

Talbot leaned forward – eager, alert, confident, the very epitome of the keen tycoon-to-be. 'Exactly, Mr Harper – and a chain of motels would increase it still more. If there's no accommodation along the route, obviously the ordinary tourist won't venture out. But if he knows he can book up beforehand at conveniently-sited motels, he'll drive out hundreds of miles without a care, and enjoy the adventure . . . I may be wrong, but I see this country more or less in the same stage of development as the United States was forty or fifty years ago. In which case the sky's the limit for growth, and there are big fortunes to be made.'

'I don't think you're wrong,' Harper said. 'We've a tremendous future ahead of us, there's no question about it . . . Mind you, for the pioneer there are always risks.'

Talbot smiled. 'Of course . . . But all business is a bet – and my company is used to risks. We thrive on them.'

'Well, it's good to know someone in the Old Country is still prepared to take a few chances. And if you decide to press on with your project, you can certainly count on the warmest support from official quarters here. As well as any detailed assistance we can give . . . What are your immediate plans?'

'I'd like to do as much on-the-spot investigation as possible while I'm here,' Talbot said. 'I thought of driving north to Townsville – for the pleasure of seeing the coastal strip and what's going on there – and then cutting right across the State to Mount Isa, and back home via Darwin. That way I'd get some idea of the road and traffic situation and the attractions of the country, and I'd hope to prospect a few nodal points for possible sites.'

'An interesting trip, Mr Talbot ... Of course, you've left it a little late in the year – you may find yourself caught in the wet before you reach Darwin. But as long as you stick to the bitumen you shouldn't come to any harm. What are you driving?'

'A motor caravan – I find it easier to manoeuvre than a car and trailer, and it's just as commodious. Naturally I expect the journey to be fairly gruelling – I've done my homework on the route and the sort of conditions I'll meet – but I'm sure it will be productive. I'm looking forward to it.'

Harper nodded. 'At your age I'd have enjoyed it too.' He pushed back his chair as Talbot rose. 'Well, it's been most pleasant to meet you, Mr Talbot ... Good luck to your prospecting, have a good trip – and we'll hope to hear more of your plans later.' He shook hands again. 'Don't forget to take plenty of petrol with you. You'll find the filling stations are few and far between once you leave the coast.'

'Thank you,' Talbot said. 'I'll watch that.'

He had, in fact, done his homework very thoroughly indeed – first back in England with Dawes, whose practical advice he had increasingly come to respect; and again, partly as a public relations front, with the people he'd met in Brisbane. He'd checked up on the terrain he'd be going through, the weather conditions he'd encounter, and the supply facilities he could expect. He'd taken advice on the right kind of van to buy, on the need for an awning, on the most effective form of fly screen, on the sort of clothes to wear and on the best maps and guide books for the journey. As a result of his conversations he'd had extra fuel and water tanks installed in the van, and he'd seen to it that there were enough bottled gas spares for the refrigerator and stove, that the tool kit was complete, that he had plenty of torch batteries, that his first-aid box was adequate, and that his small radio receiver would pick up all necessary stations for weather forecasts. For someone who reckoned not to be a man of action, he considered he'd done pretty well. Of the few things he still needed, he put high on the list a supply of decent French wine while he could still buy it, and some tinned foods of the less common varieties. Since he had to go on safari he was determined to make it as Sybaritic as possible. He spent his final afternoon shopping and completing his preparations.

Back in his penthouse suite at the luxury hotel he'd made his headquarters, he booked two personal telephone calls for the late evening, which would be the start of the working day in London; one to Furneval, to get the latest news of the Corporation and mention some small changes he proposed to make in the company's investment portfolio; one to Prendergast, to request the changes and have a general chat about the state of the stock market. It was important to keep in touch, and the wheels of his affairs well oiled.

As he took his shower before dinner, he reviewed with satisfaction his visit to Brisbane. It had really gone very well indeed. He had plausibly established, in the quarters that mattered, a reason for his presence in Australia and his forthcoming trip into the interior. He'd done it without committing himself to any definite course of action, and without incurring any unpleasant publicity. No one appeared to have got wind of that embarrassing, though commercially irrelevant episode with the Aston Martin, and its unfortunate consequences. No one had any doubts of his integrity. He was leaving Brisbane without a blemish on his character, and with the good wishes of one and all as a potential investor in Queensland's future.

He smiled at the thought. Some investor!

*   *   *

Early next morning he set off northwards out of Brisbane along the Bruce Highway. He was reminded at first of American roads he had seen. The route was lined with billboards, and ribbon-developed with caravan sites and filling stations and used car lots. Bert's Place advertised 'Eats' and 'Cooked pies'. There were 'nosh bars' and espressos in profusion; anyone who needed 'fish and chips fresh daily' would have no problem, and ice cream stalls were everywhere. It was, Talbot thought, a pretty crude and graceless scene, and he was thankful when the man-made ugliness thinned out a little.

The road itself was a good one by Australian standards, and once he was free of the city's sprawling suburbs the traffic was light. Those people who were on the move all seemed to be in an unruffled good temper at the wheel, which he found an agreeable change from home. Driving was on the left, as in England; the new van handled well; and as he had six days to cover the fifteen hundred miles to the rendezvous at Mount Isa, he was under no pressure. Dressed comfortably in the wise traveller's summer rig of shorts and shirt, with dark glasses against the glare, a panama hat on his head, and the window of his cab open to the breeze, he found the temperature of eighty degrees just right.

He drove all day through a lush and smiling countryside. This coastal strip of Queensland was fertile and productive, as well as very pleasant to the eye where no one had spoiled it. There were green hills and patches of woodland, grazing dairy cattle, plantations of pineapples and bananas and citrus, and – increasingly as he went north – great areas of sugar cane. The road took him over many creeks, some of them dry, as well as over placidly-flowing rivers and beside quiet lakes. Away to the west, the blue haze of the Great Dividing Range lay parallel to his route. The towns he passed through – Nambour and Gympie, Maryborough and Bundaberg were all quite small and presented no obstacle to progress. He stopped once at a trailer-stall to buy fruit and ripe avocados; and for an hour or so at midday to eat and take a rest in the shade of a big mango. Otherwise he kept steadily on, driving with mechanical ease, his mind largely occupied with the various aspects of the plan.

It was a good plan – he hadn't a doubt about that. It was so original and ingenious in its broad conception that no one would ever think of guarding against it. By now, too, it was pretty well perfect in detail, as a result of the work that he and Holt and Dawes had put into it over weeks of secret meetings. They'd foreseen, Talbot believed, every possible snag; they'd even taken account of some most unlikely contingencies. Now they had a blueprint for action which was almost as good as a licence to print money.

He thought, appraisingly, of his two henchmen. He'd come to know them pretty well during the long discussions, and he could see both their strengths and their weaknesses as co-conspirators. Holt hadn't quite the single-track approach that Talbot would have preferred – there were times when he seemed to have joined the enterprise almost as much for fun, for laughs, as for the money. Talbot wasn't absolutely sure how he'd behave if the fun stopped. Crime, after all, could be a serious business. But in general he had the makings of an excellent lieutenant. He was amenable and easy-going, he had an equable, peace-loving nature, he was quick at grasping things, and technically he knew his stuff. Which was quite a list of qualities.

Dawes, of course, was a very different character. At his best, Talbot saw him as a sound NCO-type; practical, experienced and loyal; glad to receive orders when they were available but resourceful enough when they were not. The trouble about Dawes was that he was moody. One day he'd be genial, large-hearted, tolerant; the next he'd be reserved, prickly, quick to resent any hint of criticism. Probably he had a bit of a chip. His moods weren't extreme, but they were sometimes disturbing. And of course Dawes had this thing about cops – which would need watching, together with his intake of Scotch. But fortunately he wasn't likely to meet many cops on this trip – and he'd given a grudging undertaking to go easy on the bottle. So that should be all right.

By and large, Talbot was well satisfied with both men. They were keen, they were confident of success, and they had a proper respect for himself as the brain and leader of the expedition. The three of them should make an excellent team.

He ended his first day's run just south of Rockhampton, close by a landscaped park that marked the point where the Tropic of Capricorn crossed the Bruce Highway. He was in a mellow frame of mind. He had covered nearly four hundred miles with no undue effort and was well pleased with his progress. He was pleased, too, with the behaviour of the van; with its luxury appointments which he was now going to enjoy, and with the camping spot he'd chosen beside a clump of tall and graceful gums which he believed were called stringy barks. For a while he sat out under his awning, watching with fascination the rainbow flittings of some tiny parrot-like birds with red beaks, blue heads, yellow necks and bright green plumage. Then, as dusk fell, he had another visitor – a big unkempt bird with a buff-coloured chest and poll, that flew in with an odd creaking noise, gave a raucous guffaw, and stood with its head cocked, as though waiting for an answer. His first kookaburra – the famous laughing jackass.

He watched it till it flew clumsily away. Then he went indoors, secured himself against flies and mosquitoes behind the van's gauze-covered windows and door, lit the lamps, and mixed himself a couple of martinis with ice from the fridge. When those were gone, he opened one of the half-bottles of Corton that he'd bought in Brisbane at vast expense, and enjoyed a leisurely meal of ham, avocado salad, cheese and fruit. Afterwards he strolled through the park in the warm evening air and chatted for half an hour with a man who'd migrated from Birmingham and was working in a local dairy. He talked enthusiastically of his motel project before saying good night.

The second day's journey was very similar to the first. Talbot still had the mountains on his left, the sea distantly on his right. There was only one sizeable place on his route, the town of Mackay, a picturesque and prosperous sugar centre with a smell of molasses in the air. Beyond Mackay were more canefields, mile after mile of them, and little settlements with scattered bungalows, their walls and gardens blazing with bougainvillaea and frangipani and other tropical flowers whose names Talbot didn't know. What struck him particularly was that everything in these gardens, tropical or temperate, seemed to flourish at the same time, for he could see oranges and lemons, apples and sweet corn, bananas and lettuce and strawberries, all apparently in season. It was, as the Director of Tourism had said, a thriving and favoured coast. Talbot even found himself wondering if he might not recommend a Corporation investment here, once his private finances had been set in order.

As evening approached he started to run out of the sugar country. The earth was beginning to take on a more arid look with patches of reddish grass in a reddish-brown landscape. By dusk he was at the outskirts of Townsville, nine hundred and seventy miles out of Brisbane. He was so far ahead of his schedule that he decided to stop there for a couple of nights and do a bit more trail-laying before he turned into the interior.

The town was full of holidaymakers and he had some difficulty in finding a hotel with accommodation. The one that finally took him in was adequate, but no more. The food was unimaginative; and men crashed up and down the corridors all night, shouting and whistling, so that he got little sleep. In the morning, having declined a T-bone steak and two fried eggs for breakfast, he set off on a tour of the town, driving up the red rock face of Castle Hill for a view of the harbour, and strolling coatless in the pleasant heat along the main shopping avenue, Flinders Street. There was nothing wrong, he decided, with Townsville itself – its streets were broad and shady, its palms graceful, its flowers colourful, its atmosphere bustling and exotic. Up to a point, at least. The local diet – as advertised in the restaurants he passed – seemed to consist exclusively of steak, carrots, peas and chips. And the bars were hellish – crowded with sweaty, noisy men who downed vast quantities of beer in frantic hurry. But then Talbot had never been much of a man for public bars, or beer, or the unadulterated company of males.

In the afternoon he made the business calls he'd planned, chatting to several friendly people at the Tourist Office and the Town Hall, and accepting an invitation to 'tea' – which turned out to be an early and stupefyingly heavy meal of roast beef and apple pudding – with the local president of the Hotels Association. In the late evening, after some delay, he managed to get through again to London. This time Furneval had some satisfying news for him. It seemed that his exploratory tour of Queensland on behalf of the Corporation had been reported and favourably commented on in the *Financial Times*, that the rate of deposits was still creeping up; and that against expectations, Oil Exploration had made a successful strike and were likely to resume their interest payments quite soon. Far from doing the company or himself any harm, Talbot thought, by his absence from the London scene, he seemed to be having quite a good effect on the fortunes of both!

If it hadn't been for the din around him, he'd have felt very cheerful that night. As it was, he postponed his retirement till one in the morning, marginally survived a few more hours of row and turmoil, and at first light thankfully turned his van towards the empty west.

* * *

He was driving now through rolling country with a scattering of gum trees, as the ribbon of road took him through the lower slopes of the Great Dividing Range. He paused briefly at a place called Charters Towers, a couple of hours along the route – a town that stood on a plateau among fantastically shaped hills that reminded him of Dartmoor tors. It had been a prosperous goldmining town, he'd read, in the last century, and the signs were still there – old heaps of mining waste, now overgrown with weeds, and open shafts and tunnels, and streets glittering white with crushed quartz. The place still had the solid look of the nineties, with stone buildings and cavernous stores set back under vaulted arcades. As he left the town, his gaze momentarily off the road as he eyed a group of black stockmen in tight breeches and white hats, he narrowly avoided a phalanx of child cyclists – and for a moment his heart stood still. Collision and investigation were contingencies that *hadn't* figured in the plan.

For a while he was still among low hills, cut by innumerable river beds whose remaining water was mostly confined to pools. Then, gradually, the appearance of the country changed again. The red earth took on a greyer shade. Soon he was travelling over a great plateau of rolling grassland, kept as a park, and dotted everywhere with sheep. The grass was dried up, and even the tussocks had been grazed by herbivores within an inch of the ground, but the sheep still seemed to be finding something to eat. From time to time he came across clumps of shady trees – various sorts of gums, he guessed, though he couldn't identify them. Some had their bark hanging in strips; some were banded or striped in pink and grey; some were olive green with sprays of foliage thrust upwards; some looked rather like cypresses. From one of the clumps, during a short stop, a kangaroo emerged with its joey bounding beside it. It stopped and sat up, gazing at him mildly, its nose twitching in a sensitive, deer-like face, its hands primly folded; then it hopped away for a few yards and paused again to stare inquisitively. It was, Talbot thought, one of the most trusting creatures he had ever seen, and since the species had commercial value he could well believe it was in danger of extinction in its wild form. Farther along the road he came across a bevy of emus and recalled the apt description of them he'd read in some book – 'like undertakers in black frock coats with hands in pockets'. First they stared at him resentfully – then they started to run beside the van with flapping tail feathers, touching thirty-five miles an hour before they broke away.

The weather was perfect. Not a cloud shadowed the vast emptiness of the great plain. The sky was a deep azure, that paled only on the far horizon. The air was dry. As he gazed around, Talbot found it hard to believe that it had ever rained here, or ever would.

Except in two small townships that he passed through – the pastoral centres of Hughendon and Richmond – there were very few turnings off the bitumen. Those that he saw amounted to no more than dirt tracks running off in various directions and apparently stretching away to nowhere. On the bitumen itself there was little traffic. Occasionally a car or utility would appear out of the apricot dust, and the occupants would wave and Talbot would wave back. Most of the vehicles he encountered were trucks, some of them huge, laden with foodstuffs and supplies. Once, improbably, he passed a well-filled bus, bound for distant Mount Isa. Once he met a tanker train, chugging along the narrow-gauge line that kept the bitumen company for most of its length. Apart from animals and birds, there was little else to see. The boreheads of Artesian wells; occasional banked-up reservoirs of water for the livestock on the stations, linked by bore-trains that showed up as thin green lines on the scorched ground; the distant roof of a homestead; a repair gang working on the road; a couple of men in outsize hats, mending a fence. At intervals of fifty miles or so there were settlements – but usually they consisted of nothing but a couple of dwellings, a post office and a police station. Most of the time Talbot had the emptiness to himself.

Once, along the route, he met a police car. In his sensitive state about the law he watched it slow down at his approach with faint concern. Not that he had anything to worry about. His documents were all in order. Thanks to luck rather than prevision, he even had an International Driving Licence – still valid, and acceptable from a visitor in lieu of that other one, defaced by official disqualification, which still lay in the glove box of the neglected Aston Martin. So his qualm was only momentary. The policemen in the car gave him a friendly grin and salute as they drove past.

He ended his day's run, well before sundown, in the shade of a clump of gum trees growing beside one of the round reservoirs. The trees were wide-spreading, with drooping blue-grey foliage and yellowish trunks, and as the bite went out of the sun they gave off a delicious aromatic scent which he found most refreshing after the heat and dust of the day. The only things that moved around him were a few sheep, birds, flies and clouds of grasshoppers. As he sat in the van, sipping his pre-dinner martinis with the dusk closing down and all sounds fading, it was quite an effort to believe in the reality of his enterprise. The Corporation, Furneval, Prendergast, Mount Henry – they all seemed a million miles away in time and distance. So did Dawes and Holt – though he hoped they weren't!

The trip continued to go smoothly in its final stages. The road was in better average condition than Talbot had been led to expect, and the van was still running well. He had ample reserves of water and petrol, enough to last him till the end of the enterprise if necessary, but he made a point of taking on a few more gallons at any small settlement that had a filling station, just as an excuse to introduce himself and have a chat about traffic and tourists and motels. Everyone was amiable, and no one seemed at all surprised at what he hoped to do.

The only appreciable change in the scene, as he drove westwards, was an increasing bareness and aridity. The tufts of spiny grass were browner, the scrub was poorer, the creeks that he crossed were all quite dry. As he approached Cloncurry, nearly five hundred miles out of Townsville, he encountered his first anthills – cylindrical pillars, some two feet thick and four or five feet high, built by the termites to keep themselves dry in the wet. Among the tombstone shapes, goats grazed in the sparse herbage.

He was still well ahead of his schedule and he decided to stay the night in Cloncurry, which was less than a hundred miles from the rendezvous. The place looked fairly primitive, but at least he'd be able to get a shower there. The temperature was well over ninety, and for the first time since leaving Brisbane he was aware of humidity. 'The Curry is hot,' the desk clerk joked, as he'd no doubt done a hundred times before to strangers. Talbot found it exciting as well as hot – though not for its intrinsic qualities. Once, he gathered, it had been an important mining town; now it was redeemed from insignificance only by its possession of a modern airport. Otherwise it was just a cattle centre. It consisted, as far as he could see, of a dusty wide main street, a few shabby and mostly undistinguished buildings with red, corrugated-iron roofs, some stockyards by the railway, and a large number of visiting aboriginal cattlemen in riding breeches, jodhpurs, moleskins and elastic-sided boots. The place contrived at once to be both congested and aimless, and its atmosphere was quite unstimulating. What excited Talbot was the sight of the bare granite ridges around the town, the mining country soon to be the scene of action. In Cloncurry, the plan suddenly seemed real again.

With reality came a twinge of anxiety. Dawes, in his description of the area, had said nothing about livestock –

yet it was now clear that a vast territory was given over to cattle. Talbot found that slightly worrying. Cattle usually wandered; cattle would have to be rounded up, presumably by the Australian equivalent of cowboys – those abos he'd seen around – on horseback and with dogs. Cattle meant men on the move, riding through trackless country, liable to show up anywhere at any time. Had Dawes been right when he'd said the land around Mount Henry was an empty wilderness that no one ever visited? It was a point of some importance.

At the hotel that evening, Talbot seized an opportunity to clear up the position. He was in the lobby before dinner, wondering whether to take a stroll or seek a drink, when a man nodded to him affably and said 'How y'goin'?' He was a big, bluff man, with a paunch that bulged over his breeches. He started to chat, and it soon emerged that he was a station manager. When he heard that Talbot was an Englishman on a business trip he took his arm in a friendly grasp and said, 'Come into the bar – I'll shout you a beer.' Talbot thanked him, and followed him into the crowded room. On this hot night, even he could use a beer. It arrived on the counter cold and clear and sparkling, with a head of white froth. He raised the glass to his host, took a long draught, and resumed the conversation.

The manager, it seemed, ran a station extending over some eight thousand square miles between Cloncurry and the Gulf of Carpentaria. His name was Harman, he had relations in Manchester and friends in Earls Court, and was keen to hear how things were going in England. He was also interested in Talbot's trip, which they discussed for some time. Harman wasn't as encouraging as some other people had been. 'I reckon it's a bit early for motels in these parts,' he said. 'A bonza idea for the future – but there aren't enough tourists on the roads yet. Not enough roads, either. That's how I see it, anyway.' He finished his beer. Talbot said – with a smile at the unfamiliar phrase – 'Now I'll shout you one!' When the refills came, he switched the talk to cattle. 'The town seems pretty full of stockmen,' he said. 'Is there something special going on?'

Harman shook his head. 'The town's full because it's a slack time – everyone's come in to yarn. There's nothing much doing at this season.'

'Oh? – how's that?'

'Well, we don't move cattle along the stock routes after September – there's nothing but poor straw on the pastures and the beasts are too weak to walk to the railhead. September to November are what we call the "starvation months". The cattle gather at the water-holes and troughs, and stick around there till the wet starts new growth.'

'And you leave them to it?'

'Too right, we do! You can't move around here once the rains come.' Harman grinned. 'Not without water wings.'

'So when do you round them up?'

'We start mustering for the meatworks about the end of March – that's when the ground begins to dry out. After that we keep hard at it – when the meat mobs are gone, there's mustering for branding and dipping. Then by September it's all quiet again, and the beasts are on their own. That's our year.'

'Interesting...' Talbot swallowed another mouthful of beer. 'Is it all good cattle land around here? Up in the hills, too?'

'Oh, my word, no – there's no fodder in the hills. Nothing but spinifex. The good cattle land is in the plain, down towards the Gulf. Not that it's all that good – it's not like the Mitchell grass country up on the Tableland. That's real bonza. We have a lot of cattle tick here, too ... Still, we get by.' Harman emptied his glass again. 'My shout, sport ...! What do you think of our beer?'

Talbot, much relieved by what he'd heard, and mentally apologizing to Dawes, gave a relaxed smile. 'Great!' he said. 'Just great!'

*   *   *

He left Cloncurry early next morning on the last lap of his journey, climbing westward on a new bitumen road that twisted and wound through copper-coloured hills, pocked with the debris of abandoned mine workings. He was in stark and elemental country now, dramatic alike in shape and colour, and – to the solitary traveller – slightly frightening. It was a place of endless parallel ridges, of rocky red outcrops, of dry creek beds and steep gulleys, of boulders and stones. An ancient and eroded place, growing nothing but sun-bleached spine grass and the thinnest scrub, and showing not a sign of life except for the occasional truck that hurried through it. There was a single oasis of a kind, half-way to Mount Isa and just off the road – a new mining town called Mary Kathleen that Talbot had been told about – but he didn't stop. After his six-day journey he was travel-weary, stiff from driving, longing for a taste of civilization. His interest now was concentrated on a certain high, candy-striped smoke stack that Dawes had described to him – and just after midday he caught sight of it. Half an hour later he was booked in at a fine new hotel in Mount Isa.

2

Holt had flown into Darwin, the administrative capital of Australia's Northern Territory, some two weeks before Talbot's arrival in Brisbane. Like Talbot, he had been enjoying his stay, though in a more light-hearted fashion. For him there had been no schedule of phoney business conferences, no special role to assume and sustain. He had presented himself as an ordinary tourist – a very well-heeled one, to judge by the money he was prepared to spend on sightseeing, and the opulent, air-conditioned hotel overlooking the sea, where he was staying. Being a tourist was an excellent cover – not just for his presence in Darwin, but for any trips he cared to make in the interior. A tourist, after all, was expected to tour.

Darwin was a place his shipping line duties had never taken him to, and he'd begun by giving the town itself a thorough going-over. He'd found it an agreeable holiday resort, brand new and fast growing, spread out spaciously above its cliffs, and tropically green. He'd explored the magnificent harbour and spent a nostalgic hour or two among the vessels tied up there. He'd had himself driven along the shores of the Timor Sea, where government servants lived elegantly in pricey houses. He'd observed with interest the polyglot population – the prosperous-looking Chinese with their cafés and curio shops, the Malays who in the early days had come to gather sea-cucumbers, the Japs who'd been attracted by pearls, the aborigines in their brightly-coloured sweat shirts, the children who ranged in hue from jet black to palest gold. He'd learned about the 'no-hopers' – the bums and beatniks who knocked up little shelters of poles and sacking on tropical northern beaches and lived an easy, layabout life on fruit and fish and sunshine. He'd enjoyed the warm, flower-scented air, the brilliant turquoise of the sea, the splendid riot of hibiscus and oleander and wistaria, the flitting budgies and parakeets. He'd drunk a lot of delicious ice-cold beer from frosted glasses in bars where a pair of shorts and thonged sandals were all a man required in the way of dress. He'd had some wonderful days swimming in the lagoon, amusing himself with an inflatable rubber dinghy – a necessary acquisition for the expedition, according to Dawes – which he'd paid money for, and an attractive French brunette whom he'd acquired for free. He'd had some pleasant evenings, too, in the hotel garden, romantic under the palms and the moon, listening to sweet music, sipping gin slings served by white-coated waiters with black ties and cummerbunds, and flirting with his temporary girl-friend.

But Darwin hadn't satisfied him for long. The girl had

gone back to Paris, the music had lost its melody, the hotel had suddenly seemed full of ageing guests – and he'd moved farther afield. He'd been flown off on a late-season trip to see a corroboree laid on by amenable aborigines; he'd been flown in a slightly different direction to watch a buffalo shoot; and he'd been on a short trip by truck and boat, a photographic safari, to get pictures of crocodiles in a muddy mangrove swamp in Arnhem Land. He had, in short, been extremely active – and the activity had been all the more satisfying because every expensive moment of it was being paid for by Talbot.

At the same time, he had overlooked none of the important matters that had been entrusted to him in connection with the expedition. He had bought, in one of Darwin's well-stocked modern stores, a transistorised, battery-driven tape recorder, made in Japan, and had proceeded to record the sounds of many exotic birds and beasts against the unlikely moment when anyone should ask why he'd needed it. He had also been able to acquire, because of his foresight in arranging the purchase by telephone some weeks earlier, a brand-new Volkswagen sleeping van with a comprehensive inventory of tropical equipment. Last, but very far from least, he had bought for approximately two hundred dollars one of the transceiver radio sets that Dawes had described in the cell at Wormwood Scrubs – a set that, unlike most, would enable him to get in touch with the Flying Doctor base by a change of wavelength and frequency. He had listened, with the concentration of the apparent layman, to everything the salesman had had to tell him about tuning and aerials, wattage and emergency call whistles – not wishing it to be known that radio had been his life. Subsequently, on the grounds that he was planning to drive alone into the outback and wished to maintain contact with civilization, he had obtained a temporary licence for the set from the Wireless Branch of the Postmaster-General's department – together with his own call sign, which he had no intention of using. Continuing with his homework, he had consulted the postal guide – where all radio outposts were listed as public telegraph offices – and had made a note of several call signs allotted to others, including that of the base at Mount Isa. From the same list he had been able to confirm that only one transceiver was currently licensed at Mount Henry. On that important point, Dawes had made no mistake.

At around the time that Talbot was talking to his Tourist Director in Brisbane, Holt was going through a list he'd drawn up in London in a final check of things to do, to get and to take. He still had to buy some extra food and a few clothes, but all the important small items – like thin rubber gloves, and electrician's tools – had been taken care of. The dinghy, deflated and roped up, was already in the van with its collapsible oars. So was the precious transceiver, with a good supply of spare parts and batteries. So was the tape recorder. So, to support his image, were a variety of tourist trophies such as any visitor to the Top End might be expected to accumulate – a boomerang of beautifully balanced hardwood that could kill or wound in skilled hands, a carved aboriginal burial pole decorated with elaborate designs in red and yellow ochre, a selection of bark paintings, a string of wallaby bones, a drawing of an abo 'wurly' constructed of tree branches and sacks, and a small crocodile skin. No one, seeing that hoard, could doubt the genuineness of his collector's enthusiasm. The van itself had been equipped with the customary extra tanks of water and petrol – though, like Talbot, Holt would be travelling on the bitumen all the way to his destination, and had no great anxieties about the journey. By the evening of December 2nd he was all set to leave for the rendezvous at Mount Isa, south-east in direction and over a thousand miles away by road.

He was clear of Darwin's ramshackle suburbs as the sun started on its northward arc next morning. Ahead of him, the bitumen road called the Stuart Highway stretched away in a ruler-straight line to the far horizon. The landscape was an arid wilderness of stone and sand; of thin eucalyptus scrub, blackened in places by the fires of the long dry months; of termite hills rising fifteen or twenty feet high from patches of parched yellow grass. Occasionally a live wallaby would bounce away out of his path – but more often he saw dead ones, hit by passing cars at night, and now rotting in the moist heat on the hard shoulder of the road. There was almost no traffic, and he could well believe that anyone stranded in this waste might have to wait, as he'd been told, for several hours before another vehicle came in sight. The road was in fair condition and he drove fast, anxious to put the dreary miles behind him as quickly as possible. In the first two hours he checked his pace only once – to edge his way past a rumbling monster, an enormous land train of three linked trailers drawn by a gigantic diesel truck with some sort of cow-catcher fender in front. Its destination, according to a sign on its side, was Alice Springs.

The settlements along the route – places like Adelaide River and Pine Creek and Katherine – were named boldly on the map as though they were flourishing towns, but they proved quite insignificant when he reached them. Mostly they consisted of no more than a handful of houses by a shallow billabong. One marked spot turned out to be a single water tank. Apart from the settlements there was almost nothing to lessen the deadly monotony of the scene ... A gently winding descent south of Pine Creek, with blue ranges visible far away – which made a change ... Some open forest land for a while, with a few palm trees scattered among the gums ... Thicker woodland around Katherine, with some tall mangoes and paw paws and a scattering of fruit and vegetable farms where the soil happened to be slightly less infertile ... But then there came another interminable stretch of near-desert that offered nothing to the eye but painful grit.

With some three hundred and eighty miles clocked up behind him, Holt pulled off the road at sundown near a place called Daly Waters. There he shut out the maddening flies, sprayed the van with an insecticide that nearly choked him, prepared a meal from tins, and enjoyed a tranquil night's sleep on an excellent foam rubber bed. At first light he was off again, heading for a place called Tennant Creek, where he had some important work to do. This second day's journey was if anything more arduous than the first. A wind had got up and was blowing hard from the south-east, kicking up thick spirals of dust around the van. The sun was blazing down from a cloudless sky and there was almost no shade. The heat in the Volkswagen was so intense that the metal parts were too hot to touch, and the ground, when Holt stepped out on it, scorched the soles of his feet through his shoes. Like Talbot, he found it hard to believe that rain ever fell here – though a pile of old flood wrack caught ten feet up in the branch of a dead tree offered dramatic evidence to the contrary. For the first time, Holt understood why Dawes had insisted he should buy that rubber dinghy.

The view still provided almost nothing in the way of variety. There were more tiny settlements built round shallow milk-white pools of water, and springs that had defied the drought – welcome oases of green trees and fresh herbage. But for score after score of miles the bitumen ran on through flat, desiccated, unused and totally uninhabited country, offering nothing but scanty scrub, stony creeks and beige desert. It was with a feeling of some relief that Holt reached his next staging post in the early evening.

Tennant Creek was much less than a town, but it was by far the largest settlement between Darwin and Alice Springs and it looked as though it might have several hundred inhabitants. It had grown up there in the waste land because of an earlier find of gold – its exact site determined by the presence of a permanent water hole, fringed with high trees that offered shade and picturesque relief from the harsh surrounding country. It had one long street, wide as a football pitch and lined on either side with single-storeyed galvanized iron houses, shops, cafés and milk bars. Behind the buildings was the desert. There was a church on stilts with white iron walls, the inevitable police station; a couple of small hotels; and, at the edge of the settlement, a modest new motel.

The hotels, Holt decided, looked a little primitive. The motel, which appeared to have its own generating plant, would be more comfortable. It would also be more impersonal. At a motel, you checked in, and didn't have to see anyone again until you checked out. Just the job ... This was not an evening when Holt wanted to chat to strangers.

In the seclusion of the van, he made his simple preparations for the role he had to play. He discarded his khaki bush shirt and substituted a flowered number which he wore loose over his shorts. On his head he stuck a peaked cotton cap that had come originally from Miami. He changed the sun glasses he'd been wearing for a larger and darker pair, packed a soft bag with the few things he'd need for the night, stuffed his tape recorder and a new tape into the top of the bag, slung a camera over his shoulder – and was ready.

Some half dozen travellers had already checked in, to judge by the cars and utilities in the parking space, but they all seemed to be safely tucked away in their rooms. Anyway, there was no one in the lobby when Holt entered, except for the girl behind the desk. He gave her a nasal greeting, said 'My! – it sure is hot!' said he was travelling down to Alice Springs, registered as Elliot F. Baker, of Princeton, N.J., collected his key, and without benefit or offer of porter, carried his bag to his room. It was a clean, bright and air-conditioned room, with piped music, a shower, a fridge with several bottles of beer in it, an electric kettle and a telephone. All the conveniences, in fact, that he needed.

He drank one of the bottles of beer, and took a shower. Then, refreshed and alert, he locked the outer door, unpacked his tape recorder, fixed a new tape, placed the microphone on the table near the telephone, and got to work.

He asked, first, for 'Inquiries' – from whom, after a short delay, he obtained the private telephone number of Ivor Williams, the manager of the Mount Henry mine. He put in a personal call – and one bottle of beer later, he was connected.

'Mr Ivor Williams?' he asked, placing the receiver beside the microphone and bending low to speak into the mouthpiece.

'Ivor Williams here,' said a man's voice. It was a rich voice, strong and musical and deep from the chest.

'Good evening, sir.' Holt switched on the tape-recorder and moved the microphone close to the earpiece of the receiver. 'My name is Elliot Baker – I'm an American from New Jersey. I must apologize, sir, for calling you up after office hours, but I'm on my way down from Darwin to Alice Springs, and this seemed a good opportunity to contact you. Can you spare me a few moments?' Holt's accent was hybrid, a horrible miscegenation of Boston and Brooklyn, but he guessed it would pass with Williams. Or with the desk girl – if, by any unlikely chance, she was listening.

The voice, audibly Welsh with its lilt and its carefully enunciated syllables, said, 'That's perfectly all right, Mr Baker. Will you tell me, please, what I can do for you?'

'It's like this, sir,' Holt said crisply. 'Back home in New Jersey I run a travel agency – and around July next I plan to bring out a group for an air tour round your great country. Now it's been suggested to me that my clients would be interested to look over one of your progressive new mines, and the name of Mount Henry was mentioned. Would you by any chance have facilities for showing tourists over your mine?'

There was a brief silence. Then the rich voice came through again. 'We're always very happy to show visitors around,' Williams said. 'But you must understand, Mr Baker, that we're right off the beaten track here, and the town has very limited accommodation. How many people would there be in your party?'

'I guess a full plane load, Mr Williams. I can't give you an exact figure right now – but I reckon it would be forty or fifty.'

'Ah ... Well, our little hotel wouldn't have room for that number, I'm afraid. You'd have to drive them in from Cloncurry and back again, all in one day, and it would be an exhausting ride – a hundred and twenty miles, no less ... My advice to you would be to make arrangements with Mount Isa to look over their mine. They have an airport there, and good hotels right on the spot, and they're accustomed to arranging organized tours.'

'Is that so?' Holt said. 'Mount Isa – I'll make a note of that ... You must forgive me – I'm not overly familiar with the geography of your country. But I guess I'll manage to locate the place.'

'You'll have no difficulty,' Williams said. 'Everyone knows the Isa. It's about a hundred and sixty miles from here by road – a fine modern mine. You couldn't do better than pay a visit there.'

'Well, thank you, sir,' Holt said. 'I'm most grateful to you for your advice and your courtesy. I trust I haven't troubled you unduly.'

'Not at all, Mr Baker – I'm happy to be of service. Goodbye.'

Williams hung up. Holt hung up, and switched off the tape recorder. Then he checked the price of the call with the office, so there'd be no delay with the bill in the morning. Having fixed that, he played back the conversation on the tape recorder. The voice of Williams, with the volume turned up a little, was clear enough to give him all he needed.

* * *

His route next day took him back a few miles to a junction of roads. There was a monument to the great 'Flynn of the Inland', whom Dawes had mentioned as the founder of the Flying Doctor service, and an east-going fork called the Barkly Highway. A signpost at the junction said 'Mount Isa. 401 miles.' Holt found it comforting. In mileage, at least, he was more than half way through his journey.

The new bitumen road cut through country more desolate and monotonous than anything he'd seen yet. It was an endless plain of bare earth and stunted scrub, treeless and featureless and utterly flat – a scorching furnace under a naked sun. For a hundred miles or more, as the highway skirted a red sand desert, there was not even the tiniest habitation. Traffic was almost non-existent. Only an occasional dead horse or bullock, a scattering of discarded beer bottles, and once a heap of broken windscreen glass by the roadside, showed that anything living had ever passed that way. When he stopped for the night, having travelled some two hundred miles, it seemed to him as he gazed around that he was in exactly the same place as when he'd set out on the highway seven hours before. The view, the heat, the emptiness – nothing had changed. It was a solitude that defied description – and the most unattractive camping spot he'd ever known.

Nevertheless he was in good heart that evening as he sat reviewing the situation over a cool beer before supper. To be making such a journey, even in a well-equipped van, was something of an achievement. Not everyone would have tackled it. And tomorrow, with luck, it would be over. After that, the future beckoned excitingly. The project in which he had joined was practically his ideal of a satisfying money-spinner. It was clever enough to be interesting; it presented a modest physical challenge but involved no danger; it could be executed without personal violence or unbearable tension; it required no hectic getaway at the end, its locale would be agreeable, not squalid; and if it came off it would be more lucrative than any comparable effort could be. It was really the crime *de luxe*, the playboy's dream, and Holt counted himself fortunate to be sharing in it.

He considered himself fortunate, too, in his companions. Talbot might not have the calibre ever to be a great tycoon, but he was certainly an attractive buccaneer. Holt had found many things to admire in him – his inventiveness and subtlety, his meticulous attention to detail, his complete lack of moral pretence, his quiet assertion of authority. He was a leader to respect. And then Dawes . . . There was really something rather endearing about Dawes. A slow, proud, simple man. A bit trying, of course, during his bouts of gloom, a bit bristly and aggressive sometimes – but he'd be all right as long as he was handled with care. And in practical matters he was the expedition's rock.

Whether the plot would actually work out in practice, only time would show. Holt couldn't quite share Talbot's absolute certainty about it – there were moments when it seemed too off-beat, too bizarre, to be entirely sound. But, theoretically, it should work. Even if it didn't, Holt thought, he personally would have had a fascinating trip and a lot of stimulating moments. Win or lose, he doubted if he'd regret it.

Meanwhile, he had a role to perfect. As he sat over his solitary supper, he repeatedly played back the conversation with Ivor Williams on the tape.

The final day brought some changes in the scene, all of them welcome to Holt. The main part of the desert stretch was now behind him. Soon he was crossing a corner of what the map referred to as the Barkly Tableland, the high watershed that divided the rivers flowing north to the Gulf of Carpentaria from those that flowed a thousand miles south to Lake Eyre. Not that anything at all was flowing now; the land was as arid as ever. But there were dry beds and deep gulleys that in the wet would become the headwaters of rivers. There were also tussocks of a kind of grass that Holt hadn't seen before – grass that looked as though it would make good pasture after rain. There were settlements again to break the monotony; even a small town, a drovers' town named Camooweal, with bare, dusty streets. The bitumen that had been straight for so long, began to wind and twist, and the surface of the world became less horizontal. Ridges appeared, dry red folds of hills, the rugged mineral country that Dawes had described. The ridges remained with Holt until, in the late afternoon, the candy-striped smoke stack of Mount Isa came into view.

The first thing he did on entering the town was to seek out a public telephone box. There was a minor chore he'd promised to take care of, a simple job but a vitally important one. In the box he looked up the number of the local Mount Henry office, and dialled it.

A girl's voice said, 'Mount Henry Proprietary.'

'Do you have a Mr Gregory there?' Holt asked, in a slow Australian drawl.

'Yes, he's our manager. Who's calling, please?'

'I'm looking for a Mr *Benjamin* Gregory. Is that right?'

'Oh, no,' the girl said. 'His name's not Benjamin, it's John...'

'Is he a very tall man – over six feet, with red hair?'

'My word, no – he's short and dark...'

'Oh, then it's a different Gregory I'm after – there must have been some mistake... Sorry to have bothered you.'

Holt hung up. That all seemed very satisfactory.

With his chore out of the way, he returned to the van and drove off to find the rendezvous.

3

Dawes had flown in to Adelaide, the South Australian capital, towards the end of November. Unlike Talbot and Holt he had spent no time in sightseeing, for he already knew Adelaide well from his mining days in Broken Hill, a mere three hundred miles away. It was, indeed, one of the few large urban places he didn't positively hate. A bit staid in its ways, maybe, but he knew no city in Australia with a background as splendid as the vineyard-covered slopes of the Mt Lofty range, a river more attractively set than the Torrens, or a finer ring of parkland preserved around it.

In the few days since his arrival he had concentrated almost exclusively on the preparations for his journey. Not just those that related to the success of the future plan, which were considerable. He had his own safety to think of as well. His journey to the rendezvous would not be on all-weather bitumen roads – it would be mainly over unfrequented desert tracks, requiring precautions that were more than a formality. His intention was to enjoy this trip as a well-organized adventure – not to 'do a perish' in the Never Never.

He was used to roughing it, in fact preferred it, and his arrangements included none of the luxuries of bed and board that Talbot and Holt had gone in for. With Dawes, the practical necessities were what mattered, and to hell with the trimmings. For transport he had settled on a Land-Rover – tough, reliable, and – with its four-wheel drive – comparatively easy to extricate from sand or mud. Having got his vehicle, he had planned with equal care his vital supplies and equipment. A tank holding eighty gallons of petrol, which would be more than enough to take him to his destination without a refill, and out again to safety. A couple of water tanks holding seventy gallons between them. A small winch, bolted to the Land-Rover's chassis at the back, and a long towing wire. A battery, plunger and flex for the demolition jobs he had to do. A miner's hat with a light in the front. A hurricane lamp and paraffin. A rifle for the odd prowling dingo, or snake. An axe, a spade and a pick. A comprehensive selection of smaller tools, and spares, including a second spare wheel with a heavy tread ... With that sort of inventory, he had no fears of being stranded. There wasn't a man in Australia, he reckoned, more skilled at getting a crook vehicle on the move again.

For the rest, it was just a question of laying in sufficient cans of tucker and an adequate supply of Scotch. He planned to do little cooking, and his only piece of heating apparatus was a tiny bottled-gas stove. He would sleep stretched out in the Land-Rover under a mosquito net or, if conditions were right, in a small tent on the ground. He'd done it all many times before, and he knew the drill backwards.

Unlike Talbot and Holt, he'd felt no need for an elaborate cover story. His accent and appearance would give him all the protective camouflage he required. He'd be an Aussie on the move, like hundreds of others. If anyone happened to ask where he was going, and why, he'd say he was going to look up his brother's family on a sheep station Hughendon way. Or anything. No one was likely to doubt what he said. Men rarely doubted what Frank Dawes said. Not openly, anyway.

He spent his last evening at the trotting races in Adelaide's great open-air floodlit stadium. He drank several cans of beer, and he won ninety dollars on the tote with some of Talbot's money.

At first light next day he set out for the Isa, a thousand miles away to the north-east.

His journey began in a very civilized way. The road from Adelaide to Port Augusta ran through green, hilly country, prosperous and well-populated, with cosy brick homes set in carefully tended gardens, flourishing orchards of apple and quince, and tall eucalyptus shading the highway. Dawes drove unhurriedly, enjoying the changing scene, protected from the sun by a broad-brimmed slouch hat and his own leathery skin, and perfectly comfortable in a temperature of ninety degrees plus. He contented himself with a mere two hundred miles that day, camping for the night on a quiet hillside with the head of the Spencer Gulf on his left and the three-thousand-foot mountains of the Flinders Range on his right.

The next day's drive was rougher – a mild forerunner of what lay in store. The surface of the road deteriorated, the country around grew dry and harsh, the settlements farther apart. He was heading now for the Dead Heart of the continent. In the late afternoon he came to Marree, a jumping-off place much favoured by the early pioneer explorers, where the main road turned west along the south side of Lake Eyre in the direction of Alice Springs. The township was no more than a few scattered houses set down in a flat, barren plain. From his isolated camp site that night he looked out on a waste of boulders and the sharp brown stones called gibbers. The view rather appealed to him, especially after he'd downed two large tots of Scotch. He regarded that as a reasonable ration, well in accordance with his undertaking to Talbot to lay off the grog. And in fact he felt no need of more. He was far from being a soak. The only times in the past that he'd had an urge to hit the bottle in a really big way had been when he'd been upset – and at present he was not at all upset. On the contrary, he found the hours of driving, the open-air life and the prospect of action ahead, quite soothing.

First thing next day he turned off the main road and plunged north-eastwards into the Never Never along the three hundred mile stock route that would take him eventually to Birdsville. This was the beginning of the testing time, for himself and for the Land-Rover. There was no need now to bother about keeping to the left of the road – on the unsealed Birdsville track you simply drove where the potholes and corrugations were fewest. Old, rutted wheel-tracks were a constant menace to springs; deep drifts of dust and sand frequently hampered progress. The earth, arid and bare and dead flat, shimmered with distorting heat waves. Fantastic mirages appeared and faded – high, flat-topped cliffs, great lakes, strange buildings. The only trace of vegetation beside the road was a sparse scattering of saltbush and spinifex. For hour upon hour, nothing moved except an occasional eagle in the sky. Dawes encountered only one vehicle – a road-grading machine, flattening and rolling the surface with its wide scraper and leaving ridges of earth on either side in its wake. He pulled up just beyond it, walked back and shook hands with the gang, joined them in a beer and chatted for a while – since to pass anyone by in that wilderness would have been a cause for comment and speculation. As it was, no one seemed at all surprised that he should be driving alone for a thousand miles to see his brother.

His camping site that night was by a waterhole on Cooper's Creek. A blistering wind was blowing up red dust, and the ground was so hot that a match accidentally dropped ignited at once. The clouds of flies were a pestilential nuisance. All the same, the site had many compensations. Paperbark trees along the creek, and reeds at the water's edge, were restful to the eye after the straining miles of the plain. The sunset was spectacular, one of the finest Dawes had seen in all his years of roaming. And there was even companionship of a sort. Innumerable birds came to the waterhole as the sun's rays cooled – eagles and hawks, plovers and heron, white cockatoos by the thousand, rosy galahs drinking in pairs, and later, when the moon got up, black swans. It was a bonza oasis, Dawes decided, as he tucked into his favourite dish of savoury mince and tomato sauce, and washed the mixture down with Scotch and water.

In the evening silence he allowed his thoughts to dwell cosily on the prospect of a hundred thousand pounds. He had not yet decided in detail how to spend it, but he had quite a few ideas. He would certainly travel to start with – maybe go round the world in one of those slow freighters

that carried a handful of passengers. Quiet and leisurely
. . . Then when he'd had his fill of the footloose life, he'd
come back to Aussie and settle down – buy himself a nice
homestead, not in a town but near enough to one to drive in
easily. Somewhere on the outskirts of Adelaide, maybe. He
might even take a wife and raise a family. He'd be able to
afford it with that kind of dough . . .

Not for a moment did it occur to him, as it had to Holt,
that the plan might fail. He had developed an implicit trust
in Talbot, a respect for his cleverness that bordered on rever-
ence. Talbot was always several jumps ahead of everyone
else. Talbot was so clear-sighted he could practically see
round corners. A real brain . . . And a good bloke, too. No
blowing about his own cleverness, no ear-bashing criticism
of others, no doing his block. Always quiet and cool, always
ready to listen, to take advice. Obviously he regarded Dawes
as the expedition's technical adviser. Dawes liked that . . .
Now Holt – well, by comparison Holt was a lightweight. A
bit of a funster. Didn't take anything very seriously. Except
radio – he knew his stuff there all right. And he was good
company. A decent bloke. They were all going to get on
fine together . . .

After the Cooper, the terrain became even more forbidding.
The ground beside the track was scabbed with glistening
salt islands. There were clay pans, baked hard as concrete
and scored by jigsaw cracks. There were huge sandhills
with windblown plumes, and low red ridges dotted with
bushes of withered grey, and outcrops of flat eroded rock
stark against the clear pale sky. Away to the north-west lay
the fearsome Simpson Desert, two hundred unbroken miles of
dunes where many a lost explorer had left his bones. Away to
the south-east lay Sturt's Stony Desert, a treeless waste covered with millions of gibbers. This was truly the heart of a
dead world. But the Land-Rover ran sturdily on, eating up
the miles of the rough and lonely track. By the early evening

Dawes was in sight of buildings that were not a mirage. Birdsville! There was nothing there when he reached it but a pub, a store, a post office and a police station. but its handful of inhabitants spelt the end of anxiety. This, for the moment, was civilization.

It was at Birdsville that Dawes began to think seriously about the explosive he had to get hold of. There were two ways he could acquire it – by buying it or by stealing it. Buying it wouldn't be difficult – gelignite was so widely used in outback Australia that the grey sticks and detonators could be bought almost anywhere. All he'd have to say – if he felt like saying anything – was that he was taking the stuff to some station where the boss wanted to open out a drying well. It was a good reason – no one would raise an eyebrow. Still, there was just a chance he might be remembered later, when the news broke from the Henry. Especially as he was going to need a large quantity. On the whole, theft seemed safer. And unless things had changed a great deal during his twelve months' absence he knew just the place where he could pick up all he wanted and leave no trace ...

North of Birdsville, the country gradually lost some of its harshness. Patches of bleached grass began to appear again in the stony sand, and there were more creeks with shallow billabongs in the bends. Birds, unseen since the Cooper, reappeared. Soon there were trees, bright herbage round the waterholes, plains turkeys, pigeons and kangaroos. Then the landscape changed once more. Ahead now were rocky hills and thicker scrub and the first of the termite mounds. The start of the mineral country. Dawes passed through Dajarra at the foot of the Selwyn range, ignored the turning for the Isa at Duchess, and kept going towards Cloncurry. He was on home ground now – ground he'd motored over in free weekends, ground he knew well. Late in the evening, he came to the quarry he remembered.

*   *   *

It was a large quarry, a source of hard red stone for construction work, that had been operating for years. A board at the unfenced entrance said 'Longara Granite Propty Ltd.' Dawes parked the Land-Rover a few yards beyond it, switched off his lights, and went back with a torch to reconnoitre. He'd timed his arrival well. It was a Saturday evening, and there was no one about, not even a weekend watchman. He wouldn't be disturbed. At least, not without warning. The headlights of an approaching car would show up miles away.

He went in through the entrance and shone his torch around. There were two trucks parked together on one side of the quarry floor. Close by, there was a wooden building that looked like an office. They wouldn't keep gelignite there. He swivelled his torch to the other side. Yes, that looked like an explosive store. He crossed to it. It was less a shed than a sunken pit, roofed with iron just above ground level. The approach was by steps cut down into the hard earth. At the bottom there was a stout wooden door, secured by a hinged steel hasp screwed into the wood, and a padlock. Dawes carefully examined the fastening, sizing up the job. Then, with a glance to left and right along the dark road, he went back to the Land-Rover and returned with a large screwdriver. It took him fifteen sweating minutes to get all the screws out and the door open without disturbing the padlock.

He flashed his torch inside. The store was stacked with wooden crates, twenty of them at least, familiar to Dawes in shape and size. Inside the crates, he knew, the gelignite sticks would be packed in smaller boxes, well padded against shock. And they'd be in good condition, not sweating and dangerous, for the quarrymen were experts and would take no chances. He looked around for other boxes – little ones, with detonators. Presently he spotted them, high on a shelf. He opened one, checking the contents. The detonators were an electrically operated type, the kind he needed.

He humped three of the crates to the road, one at a time, straining under the weight. He left them there, and drove the Land-Rover back to them, and stowed them under his own gear, together with the detonators. Then he returned to the store. To the casual eye, there was no sign that it had been rifled. He doubted if anything would be missed – at least not for some time, till a check was made. Gelignite crates weren't prized like gold nuggets. And if, at some point, they *were* missed, no one would be able to associate him with the theft.

He screwed the door hasp back in place. It showed slight signs of having been disturbed, but only on close inspection. Well satisfied with the job he'd done, he returned quickly to the Land-Rover and drove on to a final camp site well away from the quarry. Tomorrow he would continue on his way through Cloncurry to the Isa.

CHAPTER III

TALBOT WAS fascinated by Mount Isa. He had long known of the place, and the prosperous company that ran it, but he hadn't expected to find the development quite so impressive.

Forty years ago, there had been nothing there at all except the site – a bare flat valley between red and purple rock ridges, cut by the stone bed of the Leichhardt River that was dry for most of the year. An arid, barren place, a cauldron of heat, virtually incapable of supporting life.

Now, according to the brochure Talbot had picked up at the hotel, it had everything. A population of nearly twenty thousand, comprising forty different nationalities, housed in modern, air-conditioned homes with lovely tree-shaded gardens. A thousand-seat cinema and the largest drive-in theatre in Queensland. A swimming pool of Olympic standards set in palm-fringed lawns; three sports ovals; parks and tennis courts; a rodeo ground and a racecourse. Innumerable schools, churches and pubs; dance halls and restaurants; a shopping centre where you could buy anything; streets full of shiny cars. It was such a rich and booming town that it could afford to bring milk, fruit and vegetables from the farthest corner of north-eastern Queensland; beer two thousand miles from Melbourne; fresh fish in daily cargo planes from the Gulf of Carpentaria. From being a torrid patch of near-desert, it had become a commercial and trading centre that served an area thousands of square miles in extent.

And all this because, under the complex of poppet heads and smoke stacks, smelters and treatment tanks across the river, there lay the richest store of copper and silver, lead and zinc, in the continent. To Talbot, the speculator, the tycoon *manqué*, it was a fabulous story of achievement.

All the same, what excited him most on that Saturday evening was something quite different – the sound of a great jet flying out of the town's air terminal. For Talbot, the most important thing about Mount Isa was that it was an aerial crossroads; a place he could easily and quickly get away from when the moment came.

In the hotel bar that night, he took advantage of a temporary lull in business to seek some information from the white-coated steward about the rendezvous he was making for – and, incidentally, to spread a few facts around which would account for his going there.

'They tell me,' he said, as he paid for his second martini, 'that this town gets all its water from an artificial lake ... Is that right?'

'That's right, sir. Lake Moondarra, it's called – it supplies the town and the mine. They built a dam across the Leichhardt River, up in the hills, and filled a valley.'

Talbot's eyebrows went up in pretended surprise. 'Really ... ? To look at the river now, you wouldn't think there could ever be anything to dam.'

'Ah, it's different in the wet, sir – my word, yes. The water fairly roars down from the Tableland. They reckon they've got twenty thousand million gallons stored up there.'

'M'm – that's a lot of water ... How far away is this lake?'

'About twelve miles. It lies back off the Barkly, as you go west out of the town. There's a signpost at the turning ... You thinking of visiting it, sir?'

'I might,' Talbot said. 'I'm touring with a caravan – I've come right across Queensland from Brisbane and I've hardly seen a drop of water all the way. A lake would be a pleasant change ... Is it the sort of place I could camp for a night or two?'

'You could camp there as long as you liked,' the barman said. 'It's a holiday spot and it's got all facilities. There's swimming and sailing, and places for barbecues – everything you need. Hundreds of people go out there from the Isa at weekends.'

'Crowded, is it?'

'It does get kind of busy on Sundays – but most of the folk come back home in the evening. You'd find it pretty quiet after that – there'd only be the odd camper staying on. I reckon you'd like it – it's a bonza place.'

'Well, thank you,' Talbot said. 'I'll certainly have a look at it while I'm here.'

'You're from England, aren't you, sir?'

'Yes, from London.'

'Just taking a holiday in Aussie?'

'No, I'm on business.' Talbot glanced around in a friendly way, taking two other customers into his confidence as well. 'I'm planning to finance a chain of motels, as a matter of fact...'

He talked about motels, and his journey across Queensland, as long as anyone in the bar was prepared to listen to him – which turned out to be more than an hour. Then he went up to his room to renew contact with Furneval on long-distance. It was the last opportunity he'd have for some time.

Around ten o'clock next morning he checked out of the hotel, topped up the van's petrol tank at a self-service garage, and joined the line of cars streaming out on to the Barkly for a Sunday at the lake. The day was cloudless, the sun brilliant. Outside the hotel a thermometer was registering a shade temperature of ninety-three – but the air was dry and the heat not oppressive.

The holiday cars, many with boats roped to their roof-racks, were nose to tail on the highway, and there was no chance of missing the turning to Moondarra. Thirty minutes out of Mount Isa, the lake came into sight – a vast sheet of milky blue behind its great containing dam. Its shores, under vivid red cliffs, were lined with scattered gums, giving shade to dozens of carefully-positioned picnic tables and barbecue spots. Already there were scores of cars, utilities and vans dotted among the trees, many with tents erected beside them. Out on the lake, flotillas of sailing boats were moving idly in the light south-easterly airs; water-skiers were weaving among them behind fast motor launches; swimmers' heads bobbed everywhere. The place vibrated with the sounds of engines and transistors and the pleasanter whir of grasshoppers.

Talbot paused for a while, observing the carnival scene. Then he continued along the shore till he reached a place of comparative quiet, away from the barbecues and the campers. The time was just short of noon – which gave him about six hours till rendezvous. It was going to be a restful day, probably the last for quite a while, and he decided to make the most of it. He donned his swimming trunks and had one of the best swims of his life in the milk-warm lake. Then he mixed himself a large martini and settled down on an air bed in the dappled shade of a gum tree. From time to time he turned his binoculars on a boat or a swimmer or a bronzed girl water-skier sweeping by. But mostly he just sat and lazed, and watched the flitting parakeets in the branches above him.

People began to prepare for departure well before dusk. The sailing boats crept in, the outboard motors ceased to splutter, the transistors fell silent. As the orange sun plunged into the lake, new sounds took over – children being called from the water, car doors slamming, car engines revving, the honk of horns. Slowly the long beach emptied. By six o'clock Talbot could see no more than a dozen vehicles spread out along the shore, the nearest a couple of hundred yards away. A few shadowy figures moved among the trees, unidentifiable in the failing light.

As darkness closed in, Talbot made his own preparations. Rear and side lamps switched on; the interior of the van lit up; red curtains drawn meticulously over all the windows; the door unlatched. Just as it had been agreed in London. Then he waited, aware of tension. He had no reason to fear that either of the men would fail to show up – too much hung on the meeting for all of them. Still, this rendezvous was the first test of stamina, reliability and skill – and accidents did happen.

He wasn't kept long in suspense. At six forty-five precisely he caught the sound of footsteps. A slow, heavy tread on the stones, drawing nearer. The van door opened, and a face appeared in the light. The weather-beaten face of Dawes, creased in a huge grin. 'Well, how y'going, sport?' he said. He climbed in, and drew the door to behind him.

Talbot grasped his outstretched hand. 'Glad to see you, Frank. Nice timing!'

'Not too bad after a thousand miles,' Dawes said.

'Have a seat. Make yourself comfortable.'

'Thanks.'

'Is everything under control?'

'You bet!'

'Did you manage to pick up the explosive?'

Dawes nodded. 'Enough to blow the top off a mountain.'

'Good man! When did you get in?'

'I hit the Isa around three. Got in here about half an hour ago.'

'Any sign of Holt?'

'None that I could see.'

'Did you have a good trip?'

'Couldn't have been better.'

'What are you driving?'

'A Land-Rover . . .' Dawes gazed around the van. 'You've got yourself a bonza outfit.'

Talbot smiled. 'One has to keep up appearances . . .'

There were more sounds on the stones, more footsteps, this time approaching quickly. As the door swung open again, a voice that Talbot hadn't heard before, strong and vibrant and unmistakably Welsh, said, 'So you'd like your old job back, would you, Dawes?'

Dawes stiffened and stared. Then Holt came in, pink and cheerful, and closed the door behind him. 'Evening, Maestro. Evening, Frank.'

Dawes was still staring. 'You know, I could have sworn that was Williams. My oath, yes.'

Holt grinned. 'I told you I'd have him taped.'

'You're like a ruddy lyre bird.'

'Oh, lord – not *more* ornithology! What does that one do?'

'Imitates everything,' Dawes said. 'Barking dogs, circular saws, motor horns . . . From now on I reckon I'll call you Birdie.'

It was a cheerful and informal reunion, almost like a family gathering. There was nothing like a spell in the same cell, Talbot reflected, to make men feel at ease with each other afterwards. Always assuming that none of them had developed any morbid desire to reform . . . It was really rather like belonging to a good club.

He produced drinks – beer for Holt, a modest Scotch for Dawes, a glass of chilled white wine for himself. 'Plonk', Dawes called it derisively, unimpressed by Talbot's assurance that it was a sound Gewurztraminer. As they drank, Holt replied to Talbot's questions. Yes, he'd got the transceiver, and all the gen about call signs. Yes, he'd checked that Gregory was still the manager at the Isa office. Yes, he'd remembered the rubber dinghy. No, he'd run into no snags at all . . .

For a while, after that, the conversation flowed easily. Holt gave a racy account of his buffalo hunt and his crocodile safari and his abo trip. Dawes reminisced about the Birdsville track, and the job he'd had at the quarry. Talbot told with quiet pleasure of the motel trail he'd left across Queensland.

It was Dawes who said finally, 'Well, enough of the jabber. What's the next move, Chief?'

Talbot reached for a map and opened it out. 'First tell me this, Frank. How much notice are we likely to get of a change of weather – a change to the kind we want?'

Dawes shrugged. 'That's pretty hard to say. Maybe two or three days. Maybe less.'

'You mean it might be only a few hours?'

'Too right, it might. Some years there's a long, slow build-up, some years there's almost none. There's no telling which it's going to be till the change is almost on you.'

'M'm ... Then obviously the first thing we've got to do is move nearer the scene. I make it a hundred and fifty miles from here to Mount Henry via Cloncurry, and that's much too far for getting into action quickly.' Talbot pondered. 'What we really need are two forward positions – one, say, about thirty miles from the mine, for reconnaissance, and one quite close to it, for the actual job . . . You know the terrain, Frank – can you suggest anything?'

'I know a place close to it that'd be just bonza,' Dawes said. 'It's an old mine working – dates back to long before the Henry started up. Looks like a big cave in the hillside. There's a track up to it that gives good access from the road.'

'How far is it from Mount Henry?'

'Maybe a couple of miles. It's where the road runs through that gorge I told you about – couldn't be more convenient for us. It's just about where we'll be operating.'

'Is the cave large enough to take our vehicles?'

'Easy! It runs right back – there's stacks of room.'

'Would they be visible from the road?'

'Not if they were parked well inside. I reckon we could hole up there for a few days and be absolutely safe.'

Talbot nodded. 'It sounds just the job – though I'd like to have a look at it before we finally decide ... Now what about a first base? Any ideas on that?'

Dawes considered. 'Yes,' he said, after a moment, 'I think I know a spot that might do. It's about five miles short of the Linda railhead, on the road from the Curry. There's a dry creek bed that runs off to the left behind a hill – and there's some pretty thick scrub around. We could park there for weeks and never be seen.'

'What's the ground like? We don't want any broken springs.'

'It's rough – but it's safe enough, as long as you keep well above the creek. I never had any trouble.'

'Could we make it in the dark, do you suppose?'

'No problem at all, with good lights. I'd lead you in.'

'And you're sure it's not a place anyone else would go to?'

'Dead sure, Chief.'

Holt said, 'How is it *you* know about it, Frank.'

Dawes grinned. 'I used to take a sheila there now and again. For picnics – and so on.'

'Couldn't someone else take a sheila there, and so on? And find three vans?'

'It'd be a chance in a million, Birdie. The country's wide open – why would anyone else choose that spot? It just happened to be my pick.'

Holt nodded. 'Fair enough, cobber! I hope you left it tidy.'

Talbot folded up the map. 'Right,' he said, 'we'll make that First Base. And if it's okay with you fellows, I suggest we go tonight.'

They synchronized their watches and left the lake at two-minute intervals to avoid giving the impression of a departing convoy to the few remaining campers. Dawes moved off first, exactly at eight o'clock. Holt followed him, and Talbot brought up the rear. They ran quickly through Mount Isa, closed the gaps between them to a convenient hundred yards, and settled down to the two-hour slog through the rugged hills that Talbot and Dawes had already traversed. By ten they were dropping down from the Tableland into Cloncurry. There they turned off on a narrow, bitumen-sealed road to the north. The driving was easier now, for they were almost down on the plain. The road, running beside the railway that linked Cloncurry with Linda, was mainly flat and often straight. They crossed several dry creeks and rivers – one of them the wide bed of the Leichhardt – and passed through two or three small settlements with names that read strangely in the headlights – Quamby, and Koolamarra and Kajabbi. There was still a little traffic about, homeward bound from Mount Isa and Cloncurry, but it grew less at each township and by midnight they had the road to themselves.

It was just after one o'clock when Dawes slowed and stopped. As the other two caught up with him, he leaned out, indicating on his left the dry rock-strewn bed of a watercourse. Then he turned off the road beside it, keeping well up the sloping bank. The others followed, sticking close to his tail, grinding along in bottom gear. The ground was iron-hard, fissured with cracks, and so uneven that Talbot doubted if he'd have a piece of crockery left unbroken. Stones shot from under spinning wheels; tree branches scraped across windscreens. Large boulders loomed up in the light beams, compelling sudden diversions. Behind the hill the low eucalyptus scrub steadily thickened. Then they came upon a space, a natural clearing, and Dawes pulled up and switched off the engine. The others parked beside him.

Dawes climbed down and stood in his headlight beam, a grin of satisfaction on his face. 'Well, there you are, sports,' he said. 'First Base.'

2

Talbot was up with the sun next morning, eager to take a look round the site in daylight and check for himself that it was as safe as Dawes had said. With his binoculars slung over his shoulder he set off up the low hill that stood between the vans and the road, weaving his way through a particularly dense scrub that had clusters of trunks branching out from single roots. The thickets stirred with early-morning life. Ants carpeted the ground, brightly-hued birds flitted in the trees, flies buzzed in a cloud round his head. Once he paused, in startled unbelief, as a large goanna waddled across his path – an ugly creature built like an alligator, with thick bulldog legs and a powerful neck. Once he flushed from the bushes a wallaby with twin joeys in its pouch. Then the scrub ended and he emerged cautiously on to the hill top – a knoll of bare ground that gave him a perfect view of the surrounding country.

To the west, a mile or so away, there was a steep escarpment – a line of rocky red slopes, cut by innumerable dry watercourses and backed by a jumble of hills and valleys. To the north, perhaps five miles away, he could make out through his glasses some low buildings and sheds which he took to be the railhead at Linda. Eastwards, the view was less clear, because of the dazzling early sun. His general impression was of a flat and arid plain, grass-covered – if the straw-coloured tussocks could be called grass – and thinly dotted with stunted acacia and a species of twisty-trunked tree whose name he didn't know. He could see no homesteads, no water, and no cattle. The ribbon of road at his feet was empty. The only movement in his field of vision was provided by a slow goods train of enormous length, disappearing into the lavender distance in the direction of Cloncurry.

He retraced his steps through the scrub and continued past the camp to the dry river bed. Then he turned upstream towards the escarpment, hoping to find another viewpoint. Presently, to his surprise, he came across a billabong – a little pool of brownish water held in a bend and lined with smooth-barked, mottled gums in profuse flower. There were reeds there, and duck; a solitary heron and hundreds of small frogs. He climbed a little farther up the watercourse, and stopped, and looked back. He could see the scrub around the van site, but the vans themselves were invisible. Well satisfied with his excursion he returned to the camp. First Base, he felt, was as secure from chance discovery as any place could be.

The three men rested all that day, sheltering from the fierce heat under the van awnings, listening to transistor music turned down low, drinking mugs of tea from the boiling billy and filling up the time with an occasional snack which Dawes referred to as a 'smoke-o'. It wasn't until after the evening meal that Talbot raised the question of his proposed reconnaissance up the road to the mine.

'Tell me, Frank,' he said, 'how early in the morning do the supply trucks start moving between Linda and the Henry?'

'Around eight,' Dawes said. 'That's when the drivers clock on. By nine it's a procession, up and down, and it goes on till just before dusk. Most days, anyway.'

'I see... So if I left here at first light, I'd be up to your cave and back again before the traffic got moving?'

'Easy. It's only twenty-five miles.'

'Would I meet anything at all?'

'Maybe the odd car. Nothing else.'

'How about Linda? Would people be on the move there?'

'You don't have to worry about Linda – the road to the Henry turns off just before you reach it.'

'Fine... Right, then I think I'll go tomorrow – the sooner we're ready for a quick move, the better. And I'll take the Land-Rover, if that's okay with you. The vans are too conspicuous in daylight – especially mine. I've got to keep that under wraps at all costs while I'm round here.'

'Sure, Chief... Will Birdie be going along with you?'

Talbot nodded. 'I'm not doubting your judgement, Frank, for a moment – but I think we'd both like to do a recce before we commit ourselves.'

'Suits me,' Dawes said amiably. 'You're the boss . . . I'll have a nice lie-in.'

They were away next day as soon as the sky paled. Holt was at the wheel of the Land-Rover. Talbot had borrowed Dawes' slouch hat; Holt's had an even broader brim. Both men wore the hats tilted to the backs of their heads, in the fashion of the country. Both were beginning to grow a disguising fringe of whisker. They looked, Dawes said, just like a couple of fossicking Aussies – which sounded strangely derogatory coming from him, till he explained that the word meant prospecting for gems.

It took them only a few minutes to reach the outskirts of Linda. The railhead, observed from a slight rise, proved to be hardly a settlement at all. It was more a marshalling area and dump; a waste of corrugated iron sheds, stockyards, truck sidings, loading platforms, cranes, scrap metal and junk, with a mere dozen houses strung out along the highway at one end and an airstrip with a windsock at the other. The road to the west turned off just short of the airstrip. It was a broad road, well-sealed and well-maintained; money had obviously been lavished on it. A large sign at the junction said, 'Mt Henry Pty Ltd. 20 miles'.

Ahead of them now was the winding route up the escarpment that Dawes had called the 'jump-up'. The road left the level plain abruptly, climbing some hundreds of feet through jagged red rocks and continuing up a broad valley alongside a boulder-strewn river-bed that looked as though nothing had flowed in it for decades. At the head of the valley, dark ranges were visible against the skyline; on either side there was a tangle of dissected hills and ridges, enclosing areas of flatter ground between. A few trees grew beside the river – stout-boled paperbarks, and screw pines with branches like candelabra, and stark white ghost gums. Up in the hills the vegetation consisted solely of eucalyptus and acacia scrub, dense in places, and silvery spinifex grass. The only sign of man's activity, apart from the bitumen itself, was a line of short poles that carried two strands of telephone wire beside the road.

Gradually, as the Land-Rover climbed through the tumbling crags and ridges, the valley narrowed. Steepsided hills steadily closed in on it until, some fifteen miles out of Linda, it entered the gorge that Dawes had spoken of. Here, the splendidly-engineered road had in places been quarried out of solid rock. Holt began to watch the corners carefully, though no other traffic had yet appeared. Talbot looked ahead, and around, and back along the route they'd traversed, considering all the time the practical possibilities of the dramatic terrain.

Three miles on, at a sharp bend, they passed through a tight funnel of rock. The moment they emerged, Talbot spotted the old working that Dawes had called a cave. It lay well above the road on the righthand side, a gaping hole in the face of the hill. Higher up still, he could see the rusted remains of machinery, and the ruins of a building, and what seemed, from its regular shape, to be a giant heap of mining waste.

There was only one approach to the working – a track, fifty yards on, that broke back at an acute angle, climbed to the opening, and continued up to the ruins. Holt took the turning wide, swung the Land-Rover on full lock, bumped up the steep and stony track, and pulled up well inside the cave entrance.

'Nice work!' Talbot said. 'Right – let's have a bit of light.'

Holt switched on his headlamps. In their brilliant glare, the excavation was seen to be massive. Ahead, it narrowed to a tunnel, an exploring finger of the old mine, but at its widest point – the flat, rough floor in the centre – its walls were at least eighty feet apart. There was certainly room for three vehicles to park with ease.

Talbot made a quick tour of inspection, flashing a torch into several minor excavations in the walls that looked as though they'd make particularly secure camping spots. He also examined the tunnel. The working, at least near the entrance, had been hewn out of something pretty solid. It was dry and in good condition, with no roof falls, no obstructions. It sloped gently downwards in a straight line. For a moment Talbot regarded it thoughtfully. Then he walked back to the lip of the cave and joined Holt, who was studying the scene outside.

The view was most promising. To the left, the gorge narrowed sharply to the funnel they'd just driven through. To the right, it widened only a little before curving round a shoulder of hill. Between its rocky sides there was space only for the river bed, sixty feet below them, and the carved-out ledge of road, thirty feet below them. The descent of the watercourse was steep; in places its bed fell precipitously over vertical rocks. Talbot could imagine that in flood time the river here would be a series of raging cataracts. But the road engineers had obviously taken that into account when they'd built their all-weather route. The escape road would always be open.

Talbot looked at Holt. 'Well – what do you think?'

'I think it'll do very nicely,' Holt said. 'Very nicely indeed.'

Dawes was boiling up the billy on a wood fire in the clearing when Talbot and Holt got back to First Base. They joined him there, and over refreshing mugs of tea they reported on their trip. The atmosphere was one of mutual satisfaction and approval. Dawes was pleased because his choice of a forward site had found favour; the others because a major problem had been solved.

Talbot finished his tea and stretched out lazily on his air bed in the early sun. 'When do you suppose that old mine was working, Frank?' he asked.

Dawes shrugged. 'Forty or fifty years ago, maybe.'

'What were they after? The same stuff as the Henry?'

'Sure. Silver, lead, copper – anything they could sell.'

'They dug an enormous hole.'

Dawes nodded. 'They must have found something pretty rich on that hillside, to do such a big open-cast job on it.'

'They left a mountain of waste above the cave.'

'Yeah . . . A lot of it's just earth and rock they cleared away, but there are tailings, too – mullock, we call it. They must have built some sort of smelter up there – you can still see the remains. Left more good ore in that heap of waste than they took out, I shouldn't wonder. Their methods were pretty crude in those days.'

'Transport must have been a problem. Getting fuel in, and the metal out. And all the supplies.'

'No error! Where the bitumen is now, there'd have been just a track. Everything would have had to be hauled by horse teams. Some of it hundreds of miles . . . I've heard it said the first lead ore that was taken from the bed of the Leichhardt had to be hauled two thousand miles to New South to be smelted. Makes you think, don't it?'

'They were tough men,' Talbot said. He was silent for a moment. 'By the way, Frank – that tunnel at the back of the cave. How far does it go?'

'Only to the Henry.'

'The Henry . . . !' Talbot sat up smartly. 'Does anyone ever come through it? We wouldn't want to be taken in the rear.'

'No fear of that,' Dawes said. 'It was sliced in two when the Henry's main shaft was sunk. Afterwards, it was closed this side of the shaft with a wooden gate. I guess the gate's still there, if the termites haven't eaten it. Anyway, no one's ever been through the tunnel since – you can take my word for that.'

'Fair enough,' Talbot said, sensing a trace of resentment. 'I just like to check these things.'

Holt helped with a tactful switch. 'Interesting things, termites. Do they really operate underground, Frank?'

Dawes grinned. 'I wouldn't know, Birdie. But it wouldn't surprise me – they do all their work in the dark. No one's ever seen a termite in daylight.'

'Is it true they can eat through a lead pipe?'

'They can eat through anything, sport. They've even been known to tackle a billiard ball.'

'You're kidding.'

'It's a fact.'

Talbot's thoughts were still on the cave. 'Why do you suppose those chaps packed up their old working, Frank? If the tunnel joins up with the Henry, there must have been all the Henry's ore still available to them.'

Dawes shrugged. 'Maybe they got in strife when they started following the lodes down. Ventilation would have been a problem. Maybe they found the wet too much for them. Maybe they were just let down by their backers . . . There were some pretty queer birds operating in those days, specially in London. Blokes who were more interested in getting ore out of the shareholders than out of the mine.'

Talbot smiled and nodded. 'Like Horatio Bottomley?'

'Who was he?' Holt asked.

'Never heard of Horatio, Birdie? He was a company promoter – one of the most daring the City of London's ever known. He floated quite a few mining companies in Australia, back in the nineties – and he used every trick in the book. Took assays from the best ore and pretended they were average. Faked cables from the mine managers to boost his shares. Watered his capital . . . He was a top con man – larger than life, Member of Parliament, wonderful gift of the gab. A really impressive rogue. Rather a pin-up of mine, as a matter of fact.'

'What happened to him?' Dawes asked.

'Oh, he got a long stretch for fraud in the end – seven years, I think . . . There's a nice story about him – could be apocryphal, but I've always liked it. A prison visitor stopped by him when he was stitching mail bags. "Ah, Bottomley," he said, "sewing?" "No," Bottomley said, "reaping!"'

Holt gave a loud guffaw. 'Wonderful!'

'He was a good loser,' Talbot said. 'I've always been rather fond of Horatio.'

Holt, a methodical and tidy man, was clearing up his van after breakfast. As he worked, he sang, quietly and rather melodiously. Talbot, returning to the camp after a stroll, arrived in time to catch an unfamiliar quantrain, sung to a familiar Irish tune.

*'The hulks and the jails some thousands in store
But outside the jails are ten thousand times more
Who live by fraud, cheating, vile trick and foul play
They should all be sent over to Botany Bay.'*

Talbot said, 'Where the hell did you learn that, Birdie?'

'In a pub in Darwin,' Holt told him, 'one jolly Saturday night. It's known as a "Botany Bay broadside", in case you're interested. Do you like it?'

'Not frightfully good taste in the circumstances, I'd have thought,' Talbot said, with a grin.

'It's no worse than your Bottomley story, mate. All that sowing and reaping!'

'True . . .' Talbot glanced around the van. Holt's transceiver was out on a table, its telescopic aerial raised. 'Have you been trying out your machine?'

'Yes . . . I like to give it a run now and again.'

'Everything satisfactory?'

'Couldn't be better.' Holt looked at his watch. 'The morning Flying Doctor session's just starting. Would you like to hear some of it?'

'I think I would,' Talbot said. 'But keep it low.'

Holt checked that the switch was on 'Receive', and fiddled delicately with the knobs. Almost at once the set sprang into life, its loudspeaker crackling. A faint voice emerged from the static, rose to a harsh cackle as Holt turned up the volume, then settled down to reasonably human tones as more adjustments were made.

The medical calls had already begun. A man was speaking.

'... a teaspoonful of number thirty-two from the medicine chest every two hours, Mrs Saunders. Repeat, number thirty-two, three two. And one aspirin at bedtime. Over.'

'Thank you, Doctor, that's roger. I'll call you again tomorrow morning and tell you how he is. Over and out.'

The voice of another woman came on – evidently the operator in charge of the session. 'Are there any more medical calls? Over.'

'Yes, Lucy, this is Six King Peter. Are you receiving me? I'd like to talk to the doctor, please. Over.'

'I'm receiving you quite well, Mrs Jackson. Over to Dr Thorne.'

Now the doctor again. 'Good morning, Mrs Jackson. What seems to be the trouble? Over.'

'Oh dear, Doctor – Mary had a fall this morning and I think she's broken her wrist. It's terribly swollen and the poor child's crying all the time. Over.'

'I'm sorry to hear that, Mrs Jackson. Have you put a splint on it? Over.'

'Yes, I followed the instructions on the chart, Doctor. Over.'

'Well, give her two tablets of number sixteen from the chest – repeat, number sixteen, one six. That'll ease the pain quite quickly. And I'll look in this afternoon. Is your landing strip clear? Over.'

'Quite clear, Doctor – and thank you very much. Over and out...'

The medical calls went on for about ten minutes. Then the operator started on telegrams and messages.

'Calling Six Charlie Hard,' she said. 'This is Six Baker Green calling Six Charlie Hard. If you are receiving me will you please come in. Over.'

'This is Six Charlie Hard. Can you hear me, Lucy? Over.'

'I can hear you very well, Maggie, about strength five. I've got a nice telegram for you. Are you ready to write it down? Over.'

'Yes, I'm ready, Lucy. Please go ahead . . .' There was a short pause. 'I'm not receiving you, Lucy . . . Oh, sorry – I'm so excited I forgot the switch. Over.'

'Your telegram is from Adelaide and it reads, "Jennifer had daughter four o'clock this morning seven pounds three ounces both doing fine love Jack." Have you got that? Over.'

'Yes, I've got it. It's wonderful, Lucy – Jack so wanted a girl this time. Over.'

'I'm so glad, Maggie. Give them both my love when you write to them . . . Now I've a telegram for Six Horse Red. This is Six Baker Green calling Six Horse Red. If you are receiving me will you please come in. Over . . .'

The messages went on – incoming and outgoing telegrams; orders for groceries and supplies to be flown in by the weekly plane; requests for spare part for a utility, for a new battery, for a set of tyres; a special weather forecast for the area foretelling 'no change'; an inquiry about air flights from Mount Isa to Sydney. Talbot and Holt sat bent over the set, listening with a concentration that the content of the exchanges hardly merited. The messages were banal enough – but the techniques were fascinating. The acquired competence of so many simple people, the friendly efficiency of the presiding operator, the way this method of conducting the daily round was completely taken for granted, the discipline and orderliness – except once, when a heterodyne squeal showed that some person had broken into the talk and transmitted out of turn.

The two men continued to listen as the routine business ended and the galah session started. Now it was a free-for-all – yet still, in the main, orderly, with the chatter flowing almost as smoothly as though these outback people hundreds of miles away from each other were in one room and all close friends. There was chatter about the continuing drought, about cattle that had died, about what the children were up to, about some baby who'd cut two teeth, about a new litter of puppies, about the success of a cake-making, about an interesting courtship, about a forthcoming marriage . . .

'Had enough?' Holt asked. Talbot nodded, and Holt switched off.

'Well, that all came through very satisfactorily,' Talbot said. 'Loud and clear, eh . . . ? Are conditions always so good?'

'No – they vary quite a bit.' Holt lowered the aerial and packed the set carefully away in its box. 'There's not much static about today.'

'Could interference be so bad that nothing was intelligible at all?'

'It could be, but it's not very likely – especially at such short range . . . Don't worry, maestro, we'll get through. Anyway, we won't want reception to be too perfect when we spread our own glad tidings.'

'That's true,' Talbot said.

The day passed slowly. Talbot had taken account of many dangers in working out his plan, but a danger was beginning to loom at First Base that he could do little about. Boredom . . . The three men knew each other so well by now that their conversation had lost the stimulus of novelty. Some minor details of the coming action still remained to be settled, but until the weather changed there was no urgency. The chores of the camp, in however leisurely a way they were performed, took up little time. The traffic on the road during daylight was busy enough to rule out any sorties. The heat, a steady ninety degrees, was hardly conducive to exploration in the bush. And there were limits to the amount of sleep one could take. Dawes and Holt found a common interest for a while in discussing Test cricket against a background of light music on the commercial network. Talbot wandered up to his billabong at dusk, drawn by wild trumpeting sounds, and was rewarded by the sight of red and grey cranes, the Australian broglas, dancing a ballet at the water's edge. Otherwise the three men sat behind fly screens in Talbot's van, playing poker. They all liked poker – but the game was less satisfactory than it might have been since Talbot was usually the winner, and all the money they were playing for was already his.

It was at the end of an afternoon card session on the second day that Talbot, searching around for some topic that would stir up interest, said, 'Have you got that sketch of the Henry, Frank – the one you showed us in London?'

'Surely,' Dawes said. 'Like to take another dekko?'

'It might not be a bad idea to run over the salient points again . . . Let's have a little rehearsal.'

'Okay, I'll get it.' Dawes went to the Land-Rover, rummaged in his belongings, and returned in a few moments with a well-thumbed sheet of paper. Talbot spread it out on the van table and the others bent over it with him.

The sketch, which had been roughly drawn by Dawes from memory, showed the mine in section. There were four shafts, and seven levels. One of the shafts descended about three thousand feet to a mined-out area on two levels. The others served a huge producing area at depths between six and seven thousand feet.

Talbot put his finger on a point marked A, two thousand feet down, at the northern end of number two level. 'This is the place you've decided on for the break-in – right?'

'Right,' Dawes said.

'What's the estimated rate of inflow going to be?'

'Around sixty million gallons a day to start with. Working up to a hundred million gallons a day as the breach gets larger.'

'Sounds quite a cascade,' Holt said.

Dawes nodded grimly. 'My word, yes. That's a hell of a lot of water.'

'I'm trying to visualize it,' Talbot said. 'How big a hole will it need?'

Dawes considered. 'At a rough guess, I'd say something around fifteen feet in diameter.'

'Aha. Now what sort of flow can the pumps deal with?'

'About ten million gallons a day. Stepped up to maybe twenty million for a short time . . . With no other mine nearby to help draw off water, that'll be the limit.'

'So what happens?'

'What happens, sport, is that the water doors collapse under pressure, the lower pump station has to be abandoned right away, and the second pump station within twenty-four hours. Nothing can prevent it. And with no pumps operating, the whole mine will be flooded in less than a week – the storage area, the working area and all the levels below the breach.'

'Splendid . . . ! And how long before production can start again?'

Dawes shrugged. 'The breach has to be found and plugged – God knows how. Then new pumping equipment has to be brought in, the mine has to be pumped dry, all the machinery has to be replaced . . . I'd say they couldn't hope to reclaim the mine in less than a year. Maybe eighteen months.'

'All right,' Talbot said. 'Now another layman's question . . . Why are the pumps so inadequate?'

'The pumps are okay for the job they have to do in the normal way, Chief. The thing is, the Henry's known as a pretty dry mine.'

'In that case, are the experts going to believe in an accidental break-in on such a scale?'

Dawes grinned. 'They'll be staggered and no error. Specially the geologists. They'll say they never suspected there was an underground water pocket of that size. They'll say they can't understand it. Like as not, they'll blame each other for negligent surveys. But they'll believe it, all right. When you're faced with a sudden inflow of a hundred million gallons a day, you've *got* to believe it.'

'I suppose so.' Talbot thoughtfully folded up the sketch plan. 'Well, that all seems straightforward ... Oh, just one more thing. There must be no loss of life. No injuries ... Does that seem reasonable to you?'

Dawes' grin widened. 'If that's how you want it, Chief, that's how it'll be. Eh, Birdie?'

The days drifted on. Days of idle waiting, of heat and flies, of exasperated glances at the burning blue sky, of uncomforting sessions by the radio, listening to forecasts that never changed. By the end of the fourth day, Talbot was beginning to grow seriously concerned, though he tried not to show it. There was plenty of drinking water and food in the camp, enough for several weeks if necessary, but he was increasingly worried about morale. Dawes' eyes were beginning to have a bloodshot tinge in the mornings, which Talbot privately attributed to surreptitious Scotch. Holt, until now the life and soul of the party, no longer sang over his chores and showed a tendency to moon about alone. At the poker sessions, tempers flared easily. There were moments when Talbot, inexperienced in the ways of this fantastic land, wondered if the drought would ever break. Dawes had admitted there were exceptional seasons, rare but not unknown, when the monsoon arrived very late. Suppose this one was late? They could hardly hang about at First Base for more than a week or two. With nothing to occupy them, morale would collapse completely ... In sombre mood, Talbot began for the first time to contemplate the possibility of failure. Of returning to London empty-handed. If that happened, there'd be nothing left for him but flight. A quick clean-up of the illicit dollar hoard in his safe – and a long plane trip to a faraway place in a different name. What an outlook!

It was Dawes who put an end to the flap. Dawes, sniffing the air on the evening of the fifth day, his face benign at the prospect of action. 'The wind's changing,' he said. 'It's stopped blowing from the south-east.'

'Is that good?' Talbot asked eagerly.

'Sure it's good. All through the dry, it blows from the south-east, over the land. All through the wet, it blows from the north-west, over the sea. And it's changing. Look – there's a wisp of cloud up there.'

Talbot looked. 'A mere speck, Frank.'

'Okay – but it's a start. There's moisture in the air, too – I can smell it. Soon, everything'll be as hot and sticky as hell. My oath, yes.'

Talbot was unconvinced – but later in the evening the weather forecast from the local station confirmed Dawes' view. In a few days, the announcer said, the drought would begin to break.

That night, at around eleven o'clock, the three men struck camp and set off for the cave, at well-spaced intervals. They met no cars on the road to the Henry, and there were no incidents. Talbot had a little trouble with his lock at the sharp turn up the track, but he made it in the end. By midnight the two vans and the Land-Rover were safely parked in the darkness of the old working.

3

Talbot strolled to the edge of the cave and looked out. The night was bright, with a sliver of moon. Below him, in the river bed, the trunks of two ghost gums shone starkly white. To his right, above the jutting shoulder of hill, the sky glowed with the floodlights and furnaces of the Henry. He walked down the track to the road, and along it for a short distance, checking that no telltale gleam from the cave would be visible to anyone passing in a car. Then, satisfied, he made his way back to the vans.

Dawes and Holt had just unloaded the gelignite and detonators from the Land-Rover and were stacking the crates in the mouth of the tunnel, out of harm's way. Talbot lit the hurricane lamp and hung it on a hook in his van, to spare the hard-used batteries. By the time the others returned he had the place squared up and celebration drinks set out on the table.

All three men were now in the best of spirits. Their goal, the Henry, was only a couple of miles up the road. The terrain round the camp couldn't have been better suited to their purpose. The cave, cool as an air-conditioned room and kept pleasantly fresh by a current wafting up from the tunnel, was an enormous relief after the brain-dimming heat of First Base. And action, at last, was imminent...

Dawes picked up his drink. 'Cheers, you Pommies – here's luck to us all.' He drained the glass and looked cheerfully at Talbot. 'So what's next on the programme, Chief?'

'Well,' Talbot said, 'the first thing, obviously, is to take care of Henry's transceiver. Everything else depends on that. And as we may have to move fast from now on, I suggest tomorrow night for the job.'

'Sooner the better,' Dawes agreed – and Holt nodded.

'Right. Now what's the best time for the operation? Any views on that, Frank?'

Dawes considered. 'I'd say around eleven o'clock. The main rush home from the movies will be over by then, so the streets will be pretty quiet. But not empty – there'll still be a few cars around and a few folk strolling – enough for cover. If we leave it later than that, there's just a chance a car parked in the road might attract the attention of the cops.'

'All right,' Talbot said. 'Let's make it eleven... Now this can't be a one-man job – someone will have to go with Birdie, to keep a look-out and lend a hand if necessary. The question is, who?'

Holt stared at him. 'It's got to be Frank, surely? He knows where the school is. He knows the town.'

'That's true – but it's also true that the town knows him. He worked there for years, don't forget. And it's not as though you'd be operating in darkness – there'd probably be street lamps around. It would only need one of his buddies to happen along and catch sight of him, and we'd have had it ... What do *you* think, Frank?'

'You've sure got a point,' Dawes said. 'I reckon it would be safer if I could keep right out of it.'

'But how would we find the place?' Holt protested. 'Stop a passer-by and ask? "Please could you direct us to the school with the transceiver?"'

'Maybe Frank could give us verbal instructions,' Talbot said.

Dawes looked doubtful. 'You could still miss your way ...' He sat frowning. Then his face suddenly cleared. 'I know how we can work it – I'll *show* you the place. We're not more than a mile and a half from the Henry as the crow flies – less than thirty minutes on foot across country. And there's a hill that looks straight down on the town. I'll take you there, and you'll see the school and the whole layout.'

'M'm ...' Talbot pondered. He'd have preferred to have no joint sorties in daylight, now they were so close to the mine. But there were risks either way, and the choice had to be made.

'Very well,' he said, after a moment. 'As long as we make it early.'

'We'll start at piccaninny daylight, Chief. There'll be no one about in the hills, I promise you.'

'Okay – it's a date ... Now are there any other problems before we turn in?'

'Yes,' Holt said. 'It's more than a year since Frank was in the town. Has anyone thought what we'll do if the set's been moved from the school?'

Talbot smiled. 'Of course, Birdie. If we find the set's been moved, you'll drive in alone the day after tomorrow, ring up the mine office, announce in your best Australian accent that you're on a special servicing round for the manufacturers, and ask where the set is. Simple!'

'Thanks,' Holt said. 'Thanks a lot!'

Talbot was the first to wake next morning. In the cave, all was darkness – but at the entrance, dawn was breaking. He switched on the van light and looked at his watch. Five forty-five – just right. He swung out of bed, fully alert, and prepared for the sortie. The routine of rising could hardly have been simpler – minimal washing to save water, no shaving, the donning of khaki shirt and shorts, and a gulped cup of coffee. At six he rammed his panama hat on his head, shouldered his binoculars, called to the others that he'd meet them out on the hill, and went cautiously to the lip of the cave to see what the day offered.

There was no question now about the increased humidity – the air outside was like a Turkish bath. Sweat started to run the moment he emerged into it. Small insects settled in swarms on his damp flesh; flies gathered round his head. He looked up at the sky. Tiny white clouds were drifting in from the north-west. He glanced up and down the road. Nothing moved.

He climbed the stony track to the hill above the cave. The mullock heap, poised at the edge, looked more mountainous than ever at close quarters. It was a huge cone of earth and cindery rubble, streaked black and red, and almost bare of vegetation. Talbot strolled across to inspect the old ruins. They'd made a striking silhouette from the road, but close to they offered little of interest. A collapsed brick chimney; part of a wall; a few bits of rusty, unidentifiable machinery, and some disintegrating corrugated iron. Time and the termites had taken care of everything else.

In a few moments Dawes and Holt appeared. Dawes was in one of his amiable moods. His face wore the pleased look of a man about to show untutored friends round a stamping ground he knew well. 'There's just one thing to watch out for here,' he said cheerfully. 'Snakes.'

'Snakes!' Holt gave an uneasy glance around.

'Sure – they're bad in these parts. Specially the taipans. They come sliding out of cracks, right in your path. Ten feet long and aggressive as hell. They kill in a matter of minutes . . . King snakes, too – they bite like a dog and then chew at you. My word, yes.'

'Okay,' Talbot said. 'You go first.'

Dawes grinned, and set off in an easterly direction with the others close behind him. Ahead, the ground rose in a series of parallel ridges, with hollows in between. The ridges were red-brown and bare of vegetation, except for silvery pincushions of spinifex. The hollows were sparsely covered by grass that looked like hay, and had the usual scattering of spindly gums and stunted acacia, with patches of thicker, grey-green scrub between. In places there were gravelly flats, dotted with anthills that stood up like stooks in a field. Everything was bone-dry and withered and coated with dust. The only living things in sight were finches and parrots feeding off the spinifex, and hawks circling in the blue-white sky. There were many gaping cracks in the rock-hard earth – but no snakes. Dawes, in amiable mood, was a leg-puller.

The three men plodded on for twenty minutes, winding their way through the bush, keeping as far as possible to the flatter ground. Then a knobbly crag opened out before them, and Dawes called back that this was the look-out. They climbed cautiously to the top and stood, dripping with sweat, gazing down.

At their feet, cupped in a circle of harsh red ridges, lay their objective, the Henry. To Talbot it looked like a pocket-sized Mount Isa. It had the same appearance of a very modern, very spick-and-span town set down in a fiercely hostile environment. And like Isa it was divided into two parts. On the north side were the workers' bungalows, clean and smart and pleasantly sited among flower-filled gardens and shady eucalyptus. On the south side was the great complex of the mine. Between the sections lay the dry river bed, bridged at two points; and the black bitumen road.

Dawes pointed out the features. Swimming pool and sports oval; shopping area, dance hall and open-air cinema; hospital and power station; favourite pub; second favourite pub. Pipe line from a dammed reservoir built higher up the valley. Smoke stacks and head frames of the mine. Smelter and electrolytic plant. Furnaces and crucibles. Ore conveyor and crushing plant. In his reminiscent enthusiasm, Dawes seemed to have quite overlooked the damage he proposed to do around the place.

'And where's our school?' Talbot asked, with a touch of impatience.

Dawes pointed. 'There it is – just off the bitumen. The squarish building with the red tiles.'

Talbot focused his glasses on it. The school was built high up on stilts, with an area of deep shade beneath. A wide verandah, approached by a wooden stairway, ran all the way round it under a low-pitched roof. The building stood on its own, well back from the road, in a setting of tall trees, mostly gums. The road, a turning off the bitumen, was the first of several that gave access to the residential area. There would be no difficulty at all, Talbot decided, in locating the place at night, now that he'd seen it. He passed the glasses to Holt.

Holt studied the school and its surroundings with equal care, concentrating particularly on the approach from the road and the position of the surrounding trees. 'Seems a fairly reasonable proposition,' he said at last. 'Quite a bit of cover and not too many street lamps. Round the back it should be quite dark . . .' He looked at Dawes. 'Any idea where the transceiver's kept, Frank?'

Dawes shook his head. 'Not a clue, sport. But you shouldn't have much trouble finding it.'

'First I'll have to get in,' Holt said wryly. 'I'm only an amateur, remember.'

Talbot shrugged off the problem. 'Anyone can break window and slip a catch, Birdie.'

'I dare say – but breaking a window can make a lot of noise. What do we do about that?'

'You could give me a signal when you were ready – a low whistle, say. Then I'd rev the Land-Rover's engine and cover you.'

Holt grunted. 'That could bring a crowd round, too!'

'Come to think of it,' Dawes said, 'there's something else you might try. I remember now – that school's got a trapdoor in the floor and steps going up to it from the ground.'

'Really?' Holt looked interested. 'What's the idea – some sort of fire escape?'

'More likely an easy way in for supplies, I reckon. I've seen a truck parked underneath there and school chairs being passed up.'

'Won't the trapdoor be locked – or bolted?'

'I wouldn't know, Birdie. But it could be worth a dekko.'

'I'll bear it in mind,' Holt said. He returned the glasses to Talbot. 'That's about it, then.'

Talbot nodded. 'A very useful recce, Frank ... Right, let's get back to base.'

The cave was a much less restful place during the day than it had been during the night. Soon after eight o'clock the two-way traffic that Dawes had spoken of began to move along the road, dramatically changing the character of the valley. For long periods, the string of vehicles was almost continuous. There were tankers of petrol, fuel oil, milk and beer; huge trucks grinding up the gorge with containers from the railhead and the air strip; more huge trucks carrying the mine's concentrates to be loaded at Linda; and a fair sprinkling of private cars as well. At the approach to the rock funnel on the bend below the cave, every vehicle hooted. Talbot, a sensitive man allergic to prolonged noise, spent most of the day in his van, preferring the twilight of the cave's recesses to the shattering din of the highway. He was aware, for the first time since the start of the enterprise, of considerable inner tension. The night sortie to the school was not only going to be of crucial importance to the plan – it was also going to be the high spot of risk. For a professional cracksman, no doubt, the job would have seemed dead easy – certainly much simpler and safer than breaking into a house. For tyros, it was bound to be hazardous. Talbot applied his mind for some time to possible bluffs and explanations, in case any of their activities should be observed. But for once his fertile imagination produced nothing. You couldn't really offer a reasonable explanation why two total strangers should be breaking into a school in a remote mining town twelve thousand miles from home, at night – except, of course, the true one.

Sharp at ten forty-five that evening Talbot checked that the bitumen was clear of car headlights in both directions, and drove off with Holt in the Land-Rover. The two men had taken every possible precaution to make the trip a success. Their khaki shirts and shorts and wide-brimmed hats were as good a cover as clothes could provide. Both were wearing crêpe-soled sandals to deaden noise. Holt had managed to stuff into the pockets of his shorts all the bits of equipment he was likely to need – a small hammer, a knife, a set of miniature screwdrivers, a pencil torch and his rubber gloves. And the glass-smashing signal had been arranged – a parrot whistle which Holt swore was a perfect imitation of the real thing. Nothing had been left to chance.

It took them only a few minutes on the empty road to reach the outskirts of the town. Across the river bed the mine showed up spectacularly, its shaft heads and smoke stacks floodlit and its copper smelter reddening the sky with its molten glow. As Dawes had foreseen, there were still a few people about in the streets – late strollers, the odd smooching couple, the occasional homegoing car – but no one gave the Land-Rover a second glance. The geography of the town was as simple from the ground as it had been from the hill top. Talbot quickly identified the school, turned off the bitumen, and parked some fifty yards beyond the building in the darkest place he could find between lamps.

'Well, that's the best I can do, Birdie,' he said. 'It's all yours now.'

Holt drew on his rubber gloves. 'Don't worry – I'll make it somehow. Keep your ears open for the parrot!'

He waited till there was neither car nor pedestrian in sight. Then he slid from his seat, padded quickly back to the school, and dived in among the trees.

He went up on to the verandah first, and tried the front door. Predictably it was locked. He examined the windows, shielding the torch beam with his hands. All of them had the sort of catch that could be released only through a broken pane. Probably it would come to that – but not yet. He paused for a moment by the verandah rail, listening. No footsteps, no sound of engines. He returned to the ground level and made his way under the building. It was darker there, and safer. He began to move around, hands outstretched, weaving between the supporting piles. Presently his groping fingers found the steps that Dawes had mentioned. He climbed them, and felt for the trapdoor, and pressed a hand against it. As he'd expected, it was secured from the inside. Or was it . . . ? When he pressed harder, it gave a little. A small gap opened. He slid a hand through the gap and felt around. There seemed to be some sort of mat over the trap, holding it down. He climbed a step higher and got his back under the door and heaved. The gap widened. Now there was just room for him to squeeze through. With difficulty he wriggled his way under the mat, letting the trap down behind him, and in a moment he emerged, dusty and sweating, inside the school.

He found himself in total darkness, which surprised him. Some light, surely, should be coming in from the street? He groped for a wall, then for a window. The window was covered with a slatted blind. He moved to the next one. That was covered, too. They were all covered. A precaution, no doubt, against unwanted sun when the building was left empty – and very helpful, too! He switched on his torch and directed the tiny beam around him. He was in a corridor running the whole length of the building. A three-foot-wide strip of coconut matting occupied its centre. Opening out of the corridor there were four doors.

He started to explore. Two of the doors led to classrooms and one to an assembly hall with a platform at the end. There was no sign of a transceiver in any of them. The fourth door opened on to a series of smaller rooms – one furnished as an office, one of a modest staff room. Holt examined every corner. Still no transceiver. He was beginning to feel anxious now. If the set *had* been moved, they could be in real trouble. Talbot's light-hearted plan for re-locating it might be feasible – but it would take time and involve big risks. Hopefully, he continued along a short passage to another door. A store cupboard – but no radio. Round a corner – and yet another door. The head teacher's study this time, by the look of the appointments. He shone his torch around – and gave a little sigh. There, behind a big desk, was the transceiver. Bully for Dawes!

The slats of the study blind were slightly open, and he closed the chinks. Then he made a quick examination of the set. It was an older model than the one he'd bought in Darwin, but it was from the same stable and constructed in much the same way. After the homework he'd done on these transceivers, he felt he knew it as though he'd built it himself. He switched it quickly on and off, checking the current. The battery was still alive. With the pencil torch gripped in his teeth, he unscrewed the back of the set and exposed the works. For a second or two he crouched motionless behind it, identifying the wires. Then he got to work.

He worked for fifteen minutes, delicately and methodically, pausing only to brush away the sweat that poured into his eyes. When he'd finished he screwed the back of the set on again, gathered up the bits of debris that lay scattered around, made sure he was leaving everything in the room as he'd found it, and returned to the trapdoor. He stood beside it for a moment, looking uneasily at the rucked-up mat. Obviously it would be impossible for him to squeeze himself out without leaving the mat in a tell-tale bulge over the exit. And a bulge could lead to inquiries – perhaps premature discoveries...

Then a thought occurred to him. He walked round to the front door and examined the lock. It was a Yale, self-closing. He returned to the corridor and straightened out the mat. Then he left the building by the door, pulling it shut behind him. He ducked down for a moment as a car swept by with headlights blazing, waited till all was silent again, and made his way quickly to the Land-Rover.

Talbot had the door open for him. 'I was waiting for the signal,' he said. 'What happened?'

'I got in through the trap.'

'Did you find the transceiver?'

'Sure.'

'Good man...!' Talbot started the engine. 'How did the job go?'

'Piece of cake,' Holt said.

'What did you do to the set?'

'Changed a few wires round.'

Talbot grunted. 'How long will it take a radio mechanic to fix it?'

Holt grinned cheerfully in the darkness. 'No one will ever fix that set,' he said. 'When the current's switched on it'll go up in smoke!'

4

The successful sabotaging of the transceiver was a load off everyone's mind. The peak point of danger had been safely negotiated; an essential piece of the jigsaw plot neatly slotted in. The talk that night was jubilant. The way was now clear, all agreed, for work to go ahead on the next stage of the plan – preparations for cutting the road.

At sun-up next morning Dawes drove off alone in the Land-Rover for a technical reconnaissance while the valley was still traffic-free. He'd already made a provisional choice, in his own mind, of the two points where later he'd plant his gelignite, but he wanted to take a good look at the sites in daylight before he reached a final decision. One of them was about ten miles down the bitumen towards Linda, and he went there first.

The place was a bridge over a twenty-foot-wide watercourse that snaked through the escarpment and joined the valley's main river a hundred yards beyond the road. The bed of the watercourse, at present dry as tinder, was some fifteen feet deep where it passed under the road, with steep, jagged rock sides. The bridge consisted of two sheets of thick steel, each the width of the road. They were supported at either end by the rock edges of the gulley, and in the centre by three concrete pillars in a row.

Dawes climbed down into the gulley and carefully studied the structure. There were, as far as he could see, no great technical problems. Three substantial charges would bring the pillars down. A few well-placed gelignite sticks inserted into the side of the gulley at the end nearest the Henry would blow away the bolts that held the steel sheet to the rock. If the operation were skilfully carried out, the half of the bridge at the Henry end would drop into the watercourse under its own weight. And that would be that...

The longer Dawes considered the site, the more he liked it. It had one great advantage over any other – that not only motor traffic, but all traffic, would be held up. Even pedestrians. The bridge would be blown only when the monsoon was about to break. By the time the breach was discovered, the watercourse would be in roaring spate, a torrent impossible to cross . . . Of course, the collapse of the bridge would seem surprising – but to start with, at any rate, the failure would probably be put down to natural causes – the stress of traffic, the weather – rather than sabotage. Particularly as close inspection would be difficult, with most of the wreckage under water. And what was discovered afterwards wouldn't matter . . . Yes, Dawes decided, this was the perfect spot.

He drove quickly back to the cave, parked the Land-Rover inside, reported briefly on the bridge situation to Talbot and Holt, and set off on foot to prospect a site for his second road block. This one had to be at a point above the junction with the track, so that the vans would still be able to get out, and far enough off for the explosion to cause no disturbance in the cave – but otherwise as near as possible, for convenience in planting the charges.

He walked to the bend in the bitumen, fifty yards above the bottom of the track, and paused there, looking up. At that point the rocky hillside slightly overhung the carved-out road. If he could find a suitable place for the charge, it would be easy to bring about a substantial land fall there. He left the road and climbed by a circuitous route through thin scrub, studying the surface of the ground. There were plenty of cracks in the baked earth, but nothing that met his requirements. Then, almost exactly above the overhang, he came upon a cleft in the rock. It was wide at the top, narrow at the base, and about eight feet deep. He clambered down into it. Near the bottom, on the side nearer the road, there was an eroded hole, a miniature cave, in the wall of the crack. It wasn't, Dawes realized, the ideal place for a gelignite charge, since some of the blast would expend itself on open air – and he had no facilities for drilling. But it had one big point in its favour. Gelignite and detonator pushed deep into the hole would remain dry until the moment came to set them off. Preparations could be made well in advance...

He climbed back on to the hillside and stood for a moment, considering the amount of gelignite that would be needed and the quality of rock and earth that would be likely to fall when the explosion split the rock asunder. Some hundreds of tons, without a doubt – and all of it would go straight down on to the road. The fall would also tear down a telephone pole and a section of connecting wire. Two birds with one stone...

He felt well content with the sites he'd chosen as he set off back to the cave round the scrub-covered contour of the hill. Not that he was entitled to all the credit. It was true he'd picked the spots – but he had to hand it to Talbot for realizing that *two* road blocks would be necessary. Most people would have been satisfied with one good job of demolition near the cave. Dawes himself would have been satisfied with that at first. But back in London, when the plan had been no more than a sketch on the drawing board, Talbot had seen the danger. Men driving down from the Henry, and men driving up to the mine from Linda wouldn't just have stayed put with their trucks when they'd reached the road block. They'd have got past it on foot, and linked up. Not easily, in the wet – but they'd have struggled through somehow. Then they'd have exchanged news – and that would have been the end of the plot. Under Talbot's plan, they'd be held up ten miles apart, with a roaring tributary between them. And by the time they made contact, the enterprise would have succeeded. A clever bloke, Talbot...

For a while that morning, everyone was busy. Holt switched on his transceiver during the early session and picked up the local weather forecast, which warned of imminent storms. Afterwards he settled down with a pen and pad near the cave entrance to work on a script he was preparing. Talbot, having heard the forecast and observed the darkening sky, checked the tyres and oil level of his van and shaved off his whiskers, in readiness for a quick departure. Dawes had taken the hurricane lamp into the tunnel and was doing complicated things with gelignite, taping clusters of the grey sticks together like candles, methodically numbering the bundles, and measuring out lengths of wire.

The burst of energy didn't last. As the morning advanced, a creeping lassitude began to spread through the camp, and with it an odd sense of anxiety. By lunchtime the humid heat outside the cave had become so oppressive that it was a penance to approach its mouth. The light north-westerly wind had dropped completely; the air was sinister in its stillness. Slowly, the colour of the sky changed from black to purple as great peaks of cumulo-nimbus massed overhead. Soon came the first growlings of thunder, drowning the rumble of the trucks that passed and hooted on the road. The thunder grew louder and nearer; lightning flashes began to stab the darkness. A wind got up again, no longer light but roaring up the valley in terrific gusts that blew swirls of choking dust into the cave. Then, as though someone had slit open a giant cloud, the rain fell down.

Talbot had seen tropical rain before, but never anything quite like this. He sensed, rather than saw, that the trucks had come to a halt, for visibility through the streaming curtains at the cave mouth was nil, and the orchestra of thunderclaps and rushing water was deafening. The rain was so heavy that he began to fear they'd left their plan too late; that the monsoon had caught them with their preparations still incomplete. But Dawes was reassuring. This, he indicated, above the concussion of the storm, was nothing at all, a mere overture to the real thing. And he was right. In half an hour, the rain stopped as suddenly as it had started. In an hour, the sky had begun to clear.

Brief though the downpour had been, the scene outside

had changed remarkably. Water was roaring and foaming down the river bed, thick and red and dotted with flotsam. Water was sluicing down every channel of the hills and rocks. For a little while it seemed that water was everywhere. Then, as the sun blazed out again, there was a second transformation. A multi-coloured mist began to rise from the ground. The rock waterfalls thinned to a trickle and ceased to flow. The torrent pouring down the river bed perceptibly subsided. Three hours after the first thunderclap, the mist had gone and the country looked as dry as though there'd been no storm at all. Something like an inch of rain, Talbot reckoned, had fallen in less than thirty minutes – yet every last drop had run off the hard, baked ground, or evaporated, leaving not a spot, not even a dampness, behind.

The temperature had dropped only a little during the storm – from an intolerable hundred to an uncomfortable ninety – but the air at the cave mouth smelt sweeter, there was a hint of a breeze again, and the sense of lassitude had gone from the camp. Over supper the three men had a sharply practical discussion about Dawes' road block sites, and made detailed plans for the next sortie. Then, helped by a few tots of Scotch, the conversation took a lighthearted turn; Dawes got on to one of his favourite topics, the wonders of Australia. He talked of flying foxes with fifteen-foot wing spans, glider possums with webbed feet that could clear ten yards at a leap, and birds that decorated their nests with flowers and constantly rearranged them for the pleasure of it – stories that the others were inclined to take as a straight-faced leg-pull. He was moving on with gusto to 'bearded dragons' and 'spiders that barked' when Holt suddenly noticed it was transceiver time, and switched on.

The chatter at the galah session that evening was almost entirely about the weather – the number of points of rain that had fallen in different places, the awful pre-monsoon humidity, the prospects of a break. Everyone was hoping that the real wet was now at hand – and a late weather forecast again encouraged the hope. The provisional outlook, according to the announcer, was for forty-eight hours of sporadic storms, and then a longer downpour.

'That sounds pretty definite,' Talbot said, as Holt switched off. 'I think the time has come, Frank, to lay those charges.'

Dawes checked over his gear as he loaded it into the back of the Land-Rover. Three bundles of gelignite for the concrete pillars, six smaller ones for the bolts. Nine electrical detonators and nine lengths of wire. Nine polythene bags to keep out the damp, and a large ball of tarred twine. A pickaxe, and a selection of smaller tools. A miner's helmet and headlamp...

'Okay, Chief,' he said. 'I'm ready.'

Talbot climbed into the driving seat. The time was fifteen minutes short of midnight. Holt waved them off, and Talbot drove down the track and on to the bitumen. There was no traffic – there'd been none for hours. They should be safe from interruption.

They reached the bridge just after twelve. Dawes got out and unloaded his gear. Talbot drove on for fifty yards and parked the Land-Rover off the road in a patch of acacia scrub. Then he walked back to the bridge and mounted guard there, keeping a careful watch for any sign of car lights.

Dawes, his headlamp switched on, was already at work in the dried-out bed of the tributary. First he fixed three detonators to the three large bundles of gelignite, and attached wire from three coils, and wrapped the bundles in three polythene bags, and closed the necks with twine. Then, reaching up to head level, he lashed one bundle to each of the concrete pillars. At that height they'd be out of reach of any storm water that was likely to come down in the next couple of days. When the bundles were all secure, he paid out the coils of wire to the gulley bank and carried them away into the scrub to a place where a dip in the ground would provide protection from the blast at firing time.

He paused for a moment to wipe the sweat from his face. It was sweat of heat, not sweat of apprehension. He'd never felt more on top of a job. He gave Talbot a cheerful wave, and took the pick, and climbed with it up the rugged gulley wall on the Henry side. There he started to probe for cracks and soft spots, high up under the steel sheet. It was awkward work, from awkward stances, but he managed in the end to hew out six holes of adequate size. He inserted his six wrapped charges, wedged them in with bits of debris, and carried the wires away to join the others in the protective dip of ground.

It was almost one o'clock by the time he'd finished the job. It wasn't exactly a precision job and it certainly wouldn't have passed at the Henry – but in the circumstances he was satisfied. The wires, deep in the gulley, were inconspicuous. The charges would be invisible to anyone crossing the bridge in a truck. The quantity of gelignite was more than adequate for its purpose. Next time he came he'd bring the battery and plunger – and he'd be all set for the explosion.

He called to Talbot to give him a hand with the tools, and walked back with him to the Land-Rover. He sagged in his seat, exhausted by effort, as Talbot drove him back to the cave. There, for a while, he rested, refreshing himself with cans of beer. Presently, under his direction, Talbot and Holt heaved one of the two remaining crates of gelignite out of the tunnel to the cave mouth. One crate, Dawes said, would be enough for the second site. Getting it along the scrubby contour in the dark was tricky work – and lowering it safely into the crack was even more difficult. But, with the help of a rope, the three of them managed it in the end. Dawes pushed the crate into the hole, fixed a detonator to one of the sticks, and trailed the wire back through the bushes, paying it out from its reel till he had the free end deep inside the cave.

'Well, there we are, sports,' he said, breathing hard. 'Operation Gelly completed . . . Now all we need is the monsoon.'

5

As soon as they'd straightened up the camp next morning, Talbot called a script conference. Holt produced the notes he'd been working on the day before, and Talbot and Dawes went through them in turn.

Talbot was congratulatory. 'A jolly good piece of imaginative writing,' he said, as he came to the end of the document. 'And very thorough.' Then he started to raise points. 'I wonder if you're on safe ground with the form of address, Birdie? I see you've assumed that Williams and Gregory are on first-name terms. Do you think that's okay, Frank?'

Dawes shrugged. 'I can't recall that I ever heard them talking, Chief – but I guess it is. They've known each other for about five years, and there's not much starch in this country.'

'H'm – you're probably right . . . Still, there's a slight risk, and we don't want to start off on the wrong foot. I suggest you wait and let Gregory give you a lead, Birdie.'

Holt nodded. 'I'll do that.'

'And if you're to sound convincing,' Talbot said, 'there's another thing you ought to be clear on. What's the rating of the two men in the company, Frank? Who's the top one?'

Dawes considered. 'That's hard to say – they've got quite different jobs. Williams is the technical man, Gregory runs the Isa office . . . But I can tell you this – Williams is the bloke with the personality. My word, yes.'

'Then he'd probably be outspoken, tough, direct?'

'Too right, he would. He's tough with everyone, the Welsh bastard. And if he had trouble on his hands, he'd be tougher than ever.'

Talbot gave a satisfied nod. 'Good – that should help you to strike the right note, Birdie . . . Now – item three. I see you've got a query here. "Method of contact?"'

'Yes,' Holt said. 'There'll be a situation right at the beginning that I ought to know about and don't . . . Some of the key people in these transceiver areas – like the doctors – are connected with their base by landline and can speak from their homes. Do you reckon that's the case with Gregory, Frank – or would he have to be called out? The thing is, Williams would know.'

Dawes shook his head. 'Sorry, sport – I'm afraid I can't help you there.'

'Ah, well – not to worry. I'll just have to feel my way and see what happens.'

'Don't forget,' Talbot put in, 'that in any sticky patch you can always say you didn't hear properly. That'll be your "out".'

'If there's still thunder around,' Holt said, 'it'll probably be true anyway . . . Right – what's next, Maestro?'

'Item four. When you're telling about the road being blocked, you'll only be referring to the top site, of course, because that's the only one you'd be in a position to know about. But I think you might say you'd had a report from a truck driver about a dickey bridge lower down. Something to the effect that he wasn't happy about it. That would prepare them for their discovery later."

'Good idea,' Holt agreed. 'Reasonable, too, if we have a few more bad storms.' He made a note on a pad.

'Then item five. I think you might strengthen that a bit, Birdie, especially after what Frank's told us. Williams wouldn't be just worried, he'd be damned angry about everything. I know his main concern would be the situation at the mine and what to do about it, but he might well throw a word or two of blame around as well. If only to get it on the record that he wasn't responsible.'

'All right – I'll shove in a few expletives here and there.'

'Yes, let it rip a bit . . . Now item six – the most important one of all. I think the general tone's strong enough – you'll want to leave something for the booster. And the details Frank's dreamed up sound most convincing – to me, anyway. But you'd better be prepared for some technical questions you can't answer. Maybe some that even Frank can't answer.'

'I'll be ready,' Holt said. 'That's when the set will unaccountably fade. And when the trouble clears I'll just carry on with my own spiel. There shouldn't be any problem.'

'Good . . . And talking of fading, don't forget to say at some point that there's something wrong with your transceiver and you wouldn't be surprised if it packed up. That'll prepare them for the silence later.'

'Will do,' Holt said. He made another note. 'Anything else?'

'I don't think so . . . Except to wish you the best of Welsh luck!'

'Thanks. We'll cope – eh, Frank?'

'Sure,' Dawes said.

'All right.' Talbot passed the script back to Holt. 'Now let's run over the movement schedule once again. Zero hour will be at your discretion, Frank, and obviously it'll depend on the weather – but assuming the met. people stick to their forecast I imagine it'll be tomorrow evening.'

'I reckon so, Chief.'

'First of all, then, you'll clear up everything in the cave. Better do that while there's still a bit of light coming in. It's vitally important to leave nothing around you might be traced by, so do a really thorough job on it. And see that the van and Land-Rover are in good shape and ready to move off . . . The moment it's dark you'll set off the main charge. You'll check that the road's blocked and the telephone wires down. Then you'll drive full pelt to the bridge and set off the second charge . . . *After* you've crossed the bridge, of course!'

Dawes grinned. 'Yeah – that's a point.'

'From the bridge you'll carry on to our old First Base. And

at eight o'clock, or thereabouts, you'll go on the air . . .' Talbot broke off. 'Something worrying you, Birdie?'

Holt was frowning. 'I was just wondering whether that was the best order. Blowing the road first and doing the transmission afterwards.'

Talbot looked surprised. 'Why – what's on your mind?'

'Only the slight doubt about getting through with a lucid message if conditions are very bad . . . If we did the transmission first, and it failed, we could try again the next night. Once we've blown the bridge, that would be it.'

Talbot grunted. 'That's true . . . But you said the other day that you'd be able to get through in almost any conditions.'

'Oh, I think we would . . . It's just that there's all this thunder about.'

'Well, how do you rate the odds? Make a guess.'

Holt shrugged. 'Fifty to one on.'

'Then I'd say you must take the chance . . . If you transmitted first, by the time you'd done the two demolitions somebody might be on the way up from Linda to investigate – and you could run into them. That would be a much worse risk . . . What do you think, Frank?'

'I'm with you, Chief.'

'Okay,' Holt said. 'We'll stick to your arrangement.'

'Right . . . So the road's blown and you've just been on the air from First Base . . . You then beat it at top speed for Cloncurry and drive on the Townsville road for fifty miles or so, away from all the excitement. You camp out for the night in the best cover you can find, and a mile or two apart. In the morning you get together again, briefly, and Birdie puts out the booster. More or less repeating the first message but emphasizing the gravity.'

'Let's hope no one has a direction finder on us!' Holt said.

'That's not very likely – no one's going to have any suspicions at that stage . . . And there you are – the job'll be done. After the booster you'll get out of the district as fast as you can, split up, and make your separate ways home by bitumen and plane. You've got your papers, and all the dough you need. In your place I think I'd make for Brisbane, but that's up to you ... Okay?'

'Fine,' Holt said.

Dawes gave a slightly non-committal grunt. Quite suddenly, he looked as though he was sickening for one of his moods.

It was another wretchedly hot and humid day. By noon, a thermometer that Holt had placed in the shade near the cave mouth was registering a hundred and two degrees. Even the interior of the cave was beginning to feel uncomfortably sticky. In the afternoon there was a second thunderstorm, less violent than the first but much slower in moving away. Though the rain had stopped by five o'clock the sky remained dark and threatening. A weather report confirmed the previous forecast – another twenty-four hours of storms, and then the break.

As dusk began to fall, Talbot called his henchmen together for the last time. 'I think,' he said, 'the moment has come for me to push off.'

Dawes nodded glumly. 'Lucky guy!'

'I know, Frank. I'm getting out and leaving you with the chores. But I'm not going for pleasure, remember. It's absolutely vital that I get right away from the mine before the balloon goes up. After all, I will be the number one suspect when the facts come out. I'll be the man with the motive.'

'Oh, sure.'

'Anyway, I can't take the risk of being delayed in the wet. If I'm not at the end of a telephone when the news breaks, we'll have done all this for nothing.'

'I'm not arguing,' Dawes said, 'I'm just saying you're a lucky guy, that's all. We'll think about you, hitting it up in Darwin, while we're sloshing through the monsoon on the bitumen – eh, Birdie?'

'Oh, turn it up, Frank,' Holt said. 'It's what we planned from the beginning – there's no point in bellyaching . . . We'll be okay. We'll be on a good road – and we can take our time.'

'That's right,' Talbot agreed. 'Once you've finished the job there'll be no hurry at all. You've got plenty of cash and travellers' cheques. If the weather gets too foul you can always stick around in some town till it eases. If you feel like it you can fly to Sydney and whoop it up a bit before you start back. Take as long as you like – it's all the same to me . . . But whenever you do get back, you'll know there'll be a hundred thousand pounds apiece waiting for you. Don't you find that a cheering prospect?'

Dawes' expression became slightly less morose. 'I guess so, Chief . . . Anyway, what's the drill for getting in touch with you in London?'

'I was coming to that. Telephone me at the flat, any day, exactly at midnight. Ring from a call box, and hang up when I answer. The following night I'll be at the usual place with the car, usual time. That goes for both of you. Okay?'

'Fair enough,' Dawes said, and Holt nodded.

'Right. . . Now there's one other thing. I'm sure you two will get on fine when I'm gone, but just in case there are any serious differences of opinion I'm appointing you, Frank, in general charge of operations. You're the man with the seniority and the greater experience, so I think it's appropriate . . . Don't you agree, Birdie?'

'Suits me,' Holt said. 'I never did like responsibility.'

It was just after eight o'clock when Talbot drove his big van out of the cave and parked it on the track. He was looking spruce – newly washed, freshly shaved, and impeccably dressed by the best bush standards in a clean khaki shirt, clean khaki shorts and white stockings. He looked once again what he was supposed to be – a prosperous, motel-planning business man on an exploratory trip in remote parts.

'Well – so long, chaps!' he said – thinking that he sounded a bit like Sanders of the River. He grasped Dawes' hand, then Holt's. 'Good luck! Have a good journey back. And I'll look forward to your calls in London.'

He waited while Dawes walked down the track to make sure the road was clear. Then he switched on his lights, trickled down to the junction, negotiated the hairpin on to the bitumen, waved, and was off.

The night was still overcast and very dark, but the rain was holding off and his headlamps were good. He drove fast, slowing only once on the way to Linda – at the mined bridge. He knew little about gelignite, but on the whole he distrusted it – especially when it was right underneath him. He met one car just short of Linda, but in the darkness and at speed he was confident that not even the outline of the van would be remembered. Once he was past the railhead and out on the Cloncurry road, he relaxed. He was away from the dangerous Henry zone – and, for him, the worst hazards of the operation were over. No one would be able to pin anything on him now.

All the same, he felt some regret that he'd had to leave the other two to finish the job. It was obviously better if a leader could be with his men at the crunch – and he'd have preferred to stay. He'd have liked to keep a close eye on every move, right to the end. Not that he didn't trust Dawes and Holt to see the plan through – but he trusted himself more. Still, he'd had no choice. The very nature of the plot had required his early departure. Better to forget about Dawes and Holt for the time being, and concentrate on his own tricky and considerable ploy.

He made good progress on the road to Cloncurry. There was a little water over the bitumen in a few low-lying places, but not enough to impede him. He met two more cars, but they sped quickly by. The sleepy settlements along the route looked as though they'd already battened themselves down against the coming wet. In the little cattle town itself there was almost no sign of life. And beyond Cloncurry, on the rugged hill stretch of the Barkly Highway that led to Mount Isa, there was none at all.

A mile or two short of the Isa, Talbot pulled off the road for a few hours' rest. The night was hot and humid, with continuous rumbles of thunder and flashes of lightning, and he got little sleep. He rose thankfully at dawn; breakfasted at leisure; collected up the clothes and personal effects that he'd need for his journey home and a few light possessions like his binoculars and transistor radio that he was reluctant to leave behind; packed a suitcase and drove into Mount Isa just as the shops and offices were opening. His first call was at the town air terminal, where he booked a seat on a jet flight that was due to leave for Darwin at 13.35 hours.

Having made sure of his reservation, he picked on a promising-looking garage that had a row of cars and trucks lined up for sale in the forecourt, and asked if they'd like to buy his van, complete with contents. He'd been on a sort of safari, he explained once more, looking for motel sites in Queensland on behalf of his company – but now that the weather had deteriorated he'd decided to call it a day and fly home. The price he asked for the van, while not low enough to cause comment, was reasonable enough to effect a quick sale. He handed over the registration book, accepted a cheque, and had himself driven to the airport. Punctually at 13.35 hours his plane moved out on to the runway – and eighty minutes later he was in Darwin. He took a taxi to the hotel that Holt had recommended, made himself and his business known at the reception desk, rented a small but luxurious suite overlooking the sea, ordered a large martini and the latest newspapers, and sank happily into a soft chair on the balcony to catch up on the affairs of the world and watch the portents of the sky. Now it was as though he'd never been at the Henry at all.

CHAPTER IV

THE DAY that Holt and Dawes spent alone in the cave was very different in atmosphere from those that had gone before. Mainly, it was a matter of a change in Dawes. Holt didn't know whether to put it down to the withdrawal of accepted authority, to resentment over what might be considered an unfair division of labour, or to irritation caused by the high humidity and an attack of prickly heat. Whatever the reason, there was no doubt that Dawes had become much more difficult since Talbot's departure. Something was upsetting him. What was worse, he was taking comfort from repeated swigs of Scotch. The liquor had had no apparent effect on his gait or his speech, but it showed in his congested face and in an increasing truculence of manner.

At an early stage, Holt remonstrated with him. 'You ought to lay off the bottle, Frank, till the job's done. You told Talbot you would – and it's only a question of hours, now.'

Dawes gave a derisive snort. 'For Christ's sake, are you a wowser too?'

'What's a wowser?'

'A wowser's a bloody sanctimonious Puritan, mate.'

'Then I'm not one,' Holt said. 'Far from it. But I think it's daft to drink a lot of whisky at this stage. Wait till tomorrow – then it won't matter.'

'Tomorrow I won't need it. And keep your bloody advice to yourself, will you . . . If I want to grog on, I'll bloody well grog on. I know what I can take.'

'I doubt it,' Holt said. 'I can see now why you got into all that trouble with the cops.'

'Cops . . . !' Dawes' face darkened. 'Don't you talk to me about cops, sport. I might do my block.'

Holt sighed. 'I don't understand why you're going on like

this, Frank. What's the matter with you? What's eating you?' His tone was friendly, conciliatory – and it had its effect.

There was a little silence. Then Dawes said, 'I dunno, Birdie. I guess I've got a feeling. Just a feeling.'

'About the job tonight, you mean?'

'Too right!'

'I can't think why. We've made all our preparations, we've got our plans all fixed. Everything's under control.'

Dawes grunted. 'Everything except the weather – that's not under control. My bloody oath, no!'

'I don't see anything wrong with the weather, Frank. The last forecast we had gave us just what we wanted. Occasional storms till tonight – then three days of heavy rain. Exactly what we've been hoping for. What could be better?'

'Sitting in a posh hotel in Darwin could be better,' Dawes said. 'By a long bloody chalk! Out of all the strife that's coming to us . . . I tell you, Birdie, waiting around for the wet to start is getting on my bloody nerves. Specially in this bloody place . . .' He reached for his bottle of Scotch and took another swig.

To Holt's relief, Dawes retired to the Land-Rover soon after lunch and spent the afternoon sleeping. Holt himself settled down near the mouth of the cave, just out of sight of the passing traffic, and began to rehearse once more his coming role, playing over the tape of his talk with Williams to refresh his memory, and putting the final touches to his script. It wasn't exactly a peaceful place to work, with the trucks grinding by all the time and thunder rumbling among the hills, but it was better than the dark confinement of the cave. Maybe, Holt thought, that was the real cause of Dawes' trouble – claustrophobia. And very understandable, too! As a drenching shower ended, and the curtain of rain lifted from the hillside opposite, he fancied he could detect a touch of green on the brown earth. Life in this arid place was about to be renewed. It would be good to be out in the open again.

At five o'clock Dawes emerged from the shadows. By the look of him, he'd had yet another go at the bottle, but his mood had improved with the approach of action – or else he was enjoying a delayed whisky euphoria. He was amiable – indeed, almost jovial. And he got down to work with gusto, checking the petrol and oil and tyres for both vehicles and doing more than his share of clearing up the camp and packing everything away. By dusk, the only indication that the cave had ever been inhabited was the crate of gelignite still in the tunnel.

Holt shone his torch over it. 'Say, Frank – did you know this box was stamped with the name of the quarry you got it from?'

Dawes joined him, weaving a little. 'Sure, I know . . . What about it?'

'Well, do you think we ought to leave it here? If anyone happened to get suspicious about you after the getaway, and checked up on your movements, it wouldn't help that this stuff had come from a quarry you'd passed on your way. It seems an unnecessary risk.'

'Not as big a risk as taking the crate with us,' Dawes said. 'That'd be as bad as having a body in the back!'

'M'm . . . All the same, I'm sure we oughtn't to leave it.' Holt glanced towards the cave mouth. 'Look, why don't we add it to the charge at the top site? It's dark now, and the rain's stopped. It'll only take us a few minutes.'

Dawes gave a cheerful nod. 'Yeah – that's an idea. Clever of you to think of it, sport. Let's have a real bang while we're about it, eh?'

'Lend a hand, then,' Holt said.

'Don't worry – I'll hump it to the track.' Dawes chuckled, as though at some private joke. 'I'm a ball of muscle – comes of playing all those poker machines.' He heaved the crate on to his back and carried it without visible effort across the cave to the entrance. Then the two men took an end each and lugged it through the soaking bushes to the crack where Dawes had laid his charge. In a few minutes they had lowered it, coffin-like, to the bottom, and Dawes had pushed it into the hole beside the first crate.

'Good-o!' he called. He clambered up. 'Shame to waste the stuff ... Now I guess we're all set.' As they walked back together round the contour, he gave Holt's shoulder a genial slap. 'You know, Birdie, for a Pommie bastard you're quite a bright cove.'

There was a terrific crack of thunder as they reached the cave, and once more the heavens opened. They'd made it with the gelignite just in time. Now a storm was welcome, if only to cover the sound of the explosion. Holt turned the vehicles round and parked them facing the cave opening, ready for an instant getaway after the charge had gone up. Dawes crouched at the free end of his wires, attaching the battery and plunger. The time was six forty-five.

'Ready?' Dawes called.

'Hold on, Frank.' Holt went to the lip of the cave and peered out. He could see little through the screen of rain – but if there'd been headlights approaching either of the bends, they'd have shown. No one was in danger. He went back inside and stood beside Dawes. 'Okay,' he said tensely. 'Let her go.'

Dawes waited with his hand on the plunger, listening to the storm, poised for the next thunderclap. As it cracked above them, he pressed down.

The din that followed drowned the noise of the elements. First came the heavy thump of the explosion itself. Then the disintegration of the hillside, the crash of hundreds of tons of rock and earth. Then the shock wave in the valley – felt even inside the cave like a blow in the chest. All accompanied by an awe-inspiring red flash in the darkness.

Dawes straightened up, grinning. 'Whacko! That's what

I call a bonza job. Okay, let's . . .' He broke off, his grin fading. The noise was still growing. 'What the hell's that . . . ?'

From outside the cave came a mounting roar, a crescendo of sound quite different to nature from thunder or explosion or falling rock. Under their feet, the very earth seemed to be in motion. A blast of warm air swept through the cave and whistled off into the tunnel. For a long moment, both men stood as though petrified. This, Holt thought, was what an earthquake must be like. Perhaps it *was* an earthquake. He drew back in fear as a boulder bounced into the cave mouth and crashed deafeningly against the wall beside him. A stream of rubble followed it in, spreading over the floor. Incredible! Then, slowly, the noise began to subside. The air became still again, the ground ceased to shake. In a couple of minutes there was nothing to be heard but the rumble of thunder and the beat of rain.

'What was it?' Holt asked.

Dawes licked his dry lips. 'The mullock tip. It must have come down.'

They walked to the cave mouth, picking their way through scattered rocks and heaps of earth and stones, and looked out. As a flash of lightning lit the scene, they gazed upon a fearful transformation. The vast mountain of waste, shaken from its long sleep by the explosion, had poured down into the gorge like an avalanche, jamming itself in the neck of the funnel below the cave and choking the valley above it. Outside the cave, the level of the debris was several feet higher than the entrance. The river bed, the road, the track leading down from the cave – all had disappeared under the flowing mass of earth and stones and cinders.

Dawson stared at Holt. Whatever condition he'd been in an hour before, he was stone sober now.

'That's bitched us,' he said. 'We can't get the vans down to the bitumen.'

2

There was a short silence. Both men were seeking answers to problems that neither had foreseen. The problem of getting away in good order from a place that had begun to look horribly like a trap. The problem of the upset schedule – the unblown bridge, the undelivered broadcast. The problem of ultimate escape from the district...

Holt was the first to speak. 'We can still get the vans *up* the track, Frank. And the scrub at the top didn't look too bad to drive through when we were up there before.'

Dawes grunted. 'It'll be different now after the rain – and in the dark. My word, yes.'

'We'll have to manage it somehow,' Holt said. 'We've got to. There's no other way of getting the transport out.'

'That's right ... I'm just telling you it'll be a fair cow up there, that's all.'

'Perhaps we'll be able to find another way down to the road – somewhere along the escarpment.'

'Not between here and Linda, we won't – the drop's too steep for anything on wheels ...' Dawes turned and faced down the valley, as though trying to recall in the darkness the lie of the land beyond. 'North of Linda, though, I seem to remember a place – a gulley winding down the "jump-up". Pretty rough, it'd be, but I reckon we'd get down with a bit of luck. If we could make that before the wet really got started we could push through to the road there and on to the Curry. Anyway, it's our best bet.'

'What about the bridge?' Holt asked. 'If we don't blow that before the trucks start moving again, the whole plan will be down the drain.'

'Are you telling me, sport ...? We'll try and take in the bridge on the way – there'll be nothing to stop us climbing down to the road on foot when we get to the spot. Except the weather – everything depends on the bloody weather . . . We'll just have to see.'

'Okay, Frank . . . So what's the drill? Stick as close to the edge as possible without going over?'

'That's about it. As long as we keep going downhill we'll know we're not far away from the valley – everything slopes to it round here . . . Right, we'd better get cracking.'

'Yes . . .' Holt took a last look round as lightning flashed again. The waste of earth and rock was lunar in its desolation. 'Well, at least we've closed the road!' he said.

They made their preparations quickly. Dawes coiled up the wire he'd trailed over the cave floor and cut it where it disappeared under the debris and stowed it away, together with the plunger. Holt cleared aside some small boulders that blocked the exit from the cave. Then they got the vehicles over the rubble and out on to what had been the track, the Land-Rover in front. Dawes climbed in and started his engine. 'Keep close on my tail,' he called. 'If you get in any strife, bang on your horn.'

'Don't worry,' Holt said. 'I will.'

Dawes switched on his lights and moved off slowly up the track. Holt followed a few yards behind him, watching his rear lamp. The storm was still rumbling around, the rain was coming down hard, the night was black as ink between the lightning flashes. But both vehicles had good headlamps, and the short climb up the hill presented no problems. Water, streaming down the windscreens faster than the wipers could get rid of it, was a nuisance; but nothing worse.

The moment the track ended, however, difficulties began. There was no question of following even an approximately straight course, for much of the scrub was impenetrable and Dawes had to make frequent detours, looking for ways through and around it. Cross-country driving in that tangled waste was like motoring through a maze. Whenever he could, Dawes sought out the barer ground, the thinner scrub, avoiding the sodden yellow grass that could well conceal pitfalls. From time to time he bore away to the right, towards the escarpment edge, sheering off again as the gradient became too steep. The speed of the convoy, grinding along in low gear, was no more than a slow walking pace. Still, for a while, they seemed to be making good progress, weaving between the stark rock ridges, keeping to the little valleys, splashing through shallow watercourses, banging and bumping and clattering over stones and following all the time the downhill trend of the land. The ground, though streaming with rain on the surface, was still mostly hard underneath, and for several miles they suffered no serious check. Then, caught in a patch of dense scrub with no way through, they had to reverse out, and Holt's spinning rear wheels dug deep into mud. Their run of luck had ended.

It took Dawes nearly half an hour to haul the Volkswagen clear, with the help of the Land-Rover's towing wire and four-wheeled grip, and the efforts of a shoving, sweating Holt. By the end, both men were filthy with mud and grease, as wet as though they'd just emerged from a bath, and very tired. They paused briefly for a bite of food and a tot of whisky. Then, in better heart, they checked their course with the compass and set off again. Ten minutes later, Holt's van bogged down for the second time, at the bottom of a gulley, and they had another long struggle. Towing proved unsuccessful, for on the steep slope out even the Land-Rover's wheels could get no grip. After several failures Dawes jammed his vehicle behind a gum tree at the top of the gulley wall and ran out his winch wire. Soaked with sweat and half blinded by driving rain, the two men laboriously winched the van out of its morass.

For a while their rate of progress improved again as they slid and skidded down a long valley of flattened grass and sparse acacia scrub. But at the first rise they hit more trouble – and again it was the van that stuck. Brushwood, hacked from the scrub with Dawes' axe and laid as a carpet over the mud, got them clear that time – but a mile farther on the van bogged down again. And twice more, in the hour that followed, they had to resort to the winch.

By midnight, they were both exhausted. For five hours, with only one short break, they had been battling with the trackless hills, the scrub and mud, the darkness and the downpour and the heat. By Holt's speedometer they had covered thirteen miles since the start – but just how much of that was detour and where they'd finished up was anybody's guess. And at that point, neither man had any interest in guessing. They simply stopped, doused their lights, stripped off their wet clothes and fell asleep.

Dawes was wakened by silence – a sudden cessation of the rain that had been drumming on the roof of the Land-Rover all night. He looked out and saw that it was almost daylight. He struggled into his damp shirt and shorts, pulled on his gumboots, and stepped out on to the puddled ground. The thunder had passed, but the sky above was a heavy, uniform grey and there was a more ominous line of black low down on the horizon. Obviously only the briefest respite from rain could be expected – so any worthwhile reconnaissance must be carried out right away. He glanced through the window of the Volkswagen. Holt was still asleep. No point in waking him yet – a recce didn't need two.

Dawes had only the vaguest idea where they'd pitched camp, but he didn't think they could be far from the escarpment edge. With a glance at his compass, he set off through the soaking scrub. He didn't intend to go much beyond shouting distance, for fear of missing the vans on his way back. But two hundred yards on he emerged from a patch of mallee to find the top of the escarpment immediately in front of him, and the river and bitumen almost at his feet in the valley below. What was more, the place had a very familiar aspect. He glanced to his left. Half a mile away, in the grey light, he could just see the smooth platform of the bridge.

He returned quickly to the camp and woke Holt. 'Rise and shine, sport,' he called. 'We're still in business.' He reported his heartening news. 'We can be down there in fifteen minutes if we step on it – and it's too early for traffic. Let's go.'

Holt was gumbooted and ready in thirty seconds. Dawes collected the plunger, slung a coil of rope over his shoulder, and joined him.

'What's the rope for?' Holt asked.

'Busting the phone wire,' Dawes said. 'They might manage a quick link-up at the top site. A second break'll make sure they don't get through.'

He set off at top speed through the bush, with Holt close behind him. The air had cooled during the night to not much more than seventy degrees, and after the long pounding they'd taken in the vans it was quite a relief to be walking again. They had a little trouble at the escarpment edge, looking for a place to descend, but they finally found a narrow gulley cut by a stream in spate and slithered down its edge. At the bottom they crossed the stream with the 'jump-up' till they were opposite the bridge. The tributary that it spanned was now a raging river. They turned along its bank and in a few moments reached the protecting hump of ground where Dawes had left his wires exposed.

Holt lay down behind the hump. Dawes took the plunger from its waterproof bag and joined the wires to the terminals. 'Right,' he said. 'Keep your fingers crossed and your head down!' He pressed the plunger and flattened himself as the charge exploded. The flash, the roar, the rush of air were all greater than Holt had expected. Small stones and bits of debris hurtled around them. Then, as the reverberations died, they raised their heads.

'Done it!' Dawes yelled.

The bridge had fallen just as he'd hoped it would. The centre supports had shattered, the bolts at the Henry end had been torn away, and one of the steel sheets was down in the watercourse. The two men walked along the bank for a closer look. The water, they saw, was surging over the sheet with the speed and power of a mill race. Even now, with the rain barely begun, Dawes doubted if anyone could have crossed that foaming gap on foot and in safety. In a few hours, it would be impossible.

'Okay,' he said. 'One more job, and that's the lot.'

He tied one end of his coil of rope round a piece of rock and threw the rock over the twin phone wire, close to the broken bridge. Then he retrieved the loose end and, with a sudden jerk, put all his weight on the doubled rope. Somewhere along the line there was a snap, and the wires sagged gently to the ground.

Dawes turned to Holt with grim satisfaction. 'Well, that's *my* hundred thousand quid earned,' he said. 'Now it's up to you, sport.'

3

It was a little after seven-thirty when they got back to the camp. The black cloud had moved across the sky from the horizon and Holt prepared breakfast in the Volkswagen to the familiar sound of drumming on the roof. As soon as they'd eaten he got out his transceiver, set it up on the van's table, made himself comfortable beside it, and spread out his script. Dawes took up a position close by, ready to prompt him if necessary. Both men were keyed up and tense. Holt's transmission had always been seen as the climactic moment of the enterprise. Now the testing time had come.

Holt glanced at his watch. The morning session through the Flying Doctor base at Mount Isa would be well under way by now. Probably the medical calls would be over. It was a good time to break in. He checked the note he'd made of the Henry's call sign. Six Copper Dog. He switched the set to 'Receive'. There was more static and interference than on previous occasions, but a voice was audible. He made some fine adjustments and turned up the volume. The words of the speaker, though still distorted, were intelligible. It was the woman operator they'd heard before. 'This is Six Baker Green calling Six Match Peter,' she said. 'I have a telegram for you. Six Match Peter, are you receiving me? Over.'

Holt took a deep breath, switched to 'Transmit', and addressed the mike in the sonorous tone and Welsh lilt of Ivor Williams. 'This is Six Copper Dog calling Six Baker Green. Six Copper Dog calling Six Baker Green. This is an emergency . . .' A heterodyne squeal almost drowned his voice. 'Six Baker Green, are you receiving me? This is an emergency. Over.'

For a moment or two the ether was filled with a babel of words and noise. Then the operator's voice broke through, cool and efficient. 'This is Six Baker Green calling Six Copper Dog. I am receiving you. Will everyone else please keep off the air. You may listen but not transmit. I have an emergency call. Go ahead, Six Copper Dog. Over.'

'This is Ivor Williams,' Holt said. 'The manager of the Mount Henry mine. We're in bad trouble here – very bad trouble. I must speak urgently to Mr John Gregory. Have you got that – Gregory. The representative of the Mount Henry Company at Mount Isa. Over.'

'This is Six Baker Green,' the operator said. 'I am receiving you, Mr Williams. Will you please continue listening and I will try to get Mr Gregory for you.'

There was a pause. Against the background of atmospherics, indistinguishable voices rose and fell. Dawes gave Holt an encouraging nod. 'Looks like Gregory does have a phone link,' he murmured. 'That'll save us time.'

They waited in strained silence. Then the operator came on again. 'This is Six Baker Green calling Six Copper Dog. I have Mr Gregory on the line for you, Mr Williams. Please go ahead, Mr Gregory.'

A man's voice spoke. 'Hallo, Ivor. What's this about trouble? Over.'

Holt said, 'We're in a terrible mess here, John. There's been a big break of water at the northern end of number two level... Are you receiving me? Over.'

'Yes, I'm receiving you. Go ahead and give me a report. Over.'

'It happened at oh-three hundred today. Nobody knows the position exactly but a great chunk of roof or wall must have given way. We're taking water at a rate of something like sixty million gallons a day and the flow's increasing all the time. The lower pumping station's flooded...' Holt fiddled with his knobs, and the transceiver squealed. 'There's something wrong with this damned set. Are you still receiving me? Over.'

'I'm receiving you... My God, this is frightful. Go on. Over.'

'As I said, the lower station's flooded. The water doors collapsed under pressure and we had to abandon it. Now the upper one's threatened – I give it twenty-four hours at most. Anyway, it's no bloody use against this deluge – we're being overwhelmed. I've withdrawn all personnel from the mine except for the men on the top pump. Fortunately we got everyone out from the lower levels – there were some near shaves but no casualties. Over.'

'Well, that's something... Ivor, it's incredible. We've never had any report of water. How the hell could it have happened? Over.'

'It happened because some bloody boffin overlooked the biggest underground reservoir in Queensland and I hope his head rolls...! Anyway, that's the situation, and there's damned little we can do about it. The only hope is that the reservoir will run dry before long – but there's no sign of it yet. Will you report to Melbourne? Over.'

'I'll phone them right away... Listen, couldn't you try to plug four and six levels west of the main shaft? The water must be piling up in the storage area – it'll take some time to reach four and six. Over.'

Holt shot an anxious glance at Dawes. Dawes said quietly, 'Tried it. Too risky. What does he know about it, anyway?'

Holt said: 'We thought of that, John, of course – I got work started on it right away. But the water's rising so fast I had to cancel the order. We'd never finish it in time – and I can't risk men's lives. Over.'

Gregory came in again. 'Well, you know best . . . What's Faringdon's view about the break? Over.'

Holt looked at Dawes again. Dawes shrugged and shook his head. Holt twiddled his knobs. 'I didn't get that, John. You're fading badly – this set's on the blink. Over.'

'I'm receiving you all right . . . What's happened to your phone? Over.'

'I can only just hear you . . . The phone wires are down. We've had a hell of a storm – an old mullock tip's been washed down on to the road two miles below the mine, and the wires went down with it. I've sent a repair party out, but conditions are very bad. Over.'

'Does that mean I won't be able to get through on the road? Over.'

'I didn't get that, John. Will you repeat it? Over.'

'I said can I get through on the road? Over.'

'You can try, but I doubt it. I'm not too sure of the road lower down, either – the last truck driver who got through reported a bridge in a bad state . . . Look, I've got to go now. Tell Melbourne we're doing all we can, which isn't much. If this bloody set holds out I'll try to raise you again this evening and give you the latest report. Over.'

'Okay, Ivor. I'll inspect the road block during the day and if it's bad I'll get a working party on it from this end as well. Good luck! Over.'

'Thanks – we're going to need it, man. Over and out.'

Holt switched the set off, and sat back. His face was pale with effort and pouring with sweat. 'Well, that's *my* hundred thousand quid's worth . . . Now let's hope Talbot earns his lot.' He reached for a towel and mopped himself. 'Who's Faringdon, by the way? That was a bad moment.'

Dawes shook his head. 'Never heard of him, Birdie – he must be after my time. But you handled it all right – my bloody oath, yes. You did a mighty job all through.'

'Thanks,' Holt said. He began to put the set away. 'Now we'd better get the hell out of it before the rumpus starts.'

'That's right . . .' Dawes looked out of the window. The rain was still bucketing down. 'If we can . . . !'

4

Holt had none of Dawes' forebodings as he prepared to strike camp that morning. On the contrary, he was quite optimistic. The setback at the cave had been largely made good. The bridge was blown, the message had gone out – virtually, the job was done. Only the booster remained – and that could be put out from anywhere. Even if it were omitted altogether, no irreparable damage would be done. As for the physical problems of the getaway – well, it couldn't be much more than twelve miles to the gulley north of Linda where they were going to descend the 'jump-up'. That was only a little more than the distance they'd covered during the night – and they could hardly make worse progress in daylight than in the dark. Even allowing for the obscuring rain, it should be easier to avoid obstacles, to make a better choice of the route ahead. So Holt argued to himself as, hopefully, he turned the Volkswagen once more on to the Land-Rover's tail.

It took him only a few minutes to realize how misplaced his hopes had been and what a desperate struggle faced them. For the problem was to find a route at all. Watercourses which the night before had been no more than harmless trickles between boulders were now impassable torrents

– and there were dozens of them across the path, running down from the hills to feed the valley. The first thing, therefore, was to work up between the streams to much higher ground, nearer their sources. That meant miles of detour. Nor was it only a question of a longer route. After a night of steady rain the water had at last begun to soak into the baked earth and the ground had become much stickier everywhere.

In the first three hours Holt bogged down five times. Each stop involved the men in a protracted and exhausting battle before the van was extricated. Twice, the winch had to be used. The rain, though not torrential, was heavy and persistent – 'a blinding bloody nuisance', as Dawes said – hampering all their efforts. And the terrain showed no sign of improvement as they advanced. All morning they had the same unending vista of grey scrub and beaten grass, of streaming red earth and axle-threatening gulleys and boulders. By the time Dawes called a halt for lunch – with only five more miles on the clock and much of that in the wrong direction – Holt had become extremely thoughful.

'You don't suppose, Frank,' he said, 'we'd do better to hole up here for a while and let this lot of rain go over?'

Dawes shook his head, 'No, Birdie, I don't.'

'Why not?'

'Because the cops'll be after us, mate.'

'Not for a day or two, surely?'

Dawes shrugged. 'Who knows when? Nobody's going to be fooled for long into believing that bridge fell down by accident. And the guys at the bottom could link up with the guys at the top sooner than we reckoned ... I'd say the cops could start searching any time from tomorrow on. Probably with aircraft, when the sky clears. And probably right here.'

'Why here, Frank? They won't know we got shut in by the landfall. We could have had transport waiting down the road.'

'They'll soon find out we didn't,' Dawes said. 'They're

bastards, but they're not stupid. They'll see our wheel marks going up the track and on into the bush – and that's all they'll need. They'll throw a cordon round the area and they'll get us . . . I tell you, Birdie, if we're going to be safe when the penny drops, we've got to be a good hundred miles away. It's the bitumen or bust.'

Holt grunted.

'What's more,' Dawes added grimly, 'this lot of rain's going to get worse before it gets better – and by the time it's over the ground'll be too soft for moving. If we're not on a bitumen road inside twenty-four hours, we can say goodbye to anything on wheels. Maybe for weeks. So we'd better push on while we can.'

Holt gave a reluctant nod. 'I suppose you're right . . . I just wondered.'

The afternoon was a slogging repetition of the morning. Every half mile or so, one or other of the vehicles churned to a stop – and almost always it was the rear-driven Volkswagen. Rain still poured steadily from a pewter sky. Both men had long ago reconciled themselves to being permanently soaked and permanently weary – but, with the help of winch and tow-rope, they struggled on . . . Then, around five o'clock, they ran into new trouble. At a gulley crossing, Holt's van dropped heavily down the bank and a rear spring broke. The van was still mobile, but it had a drunken list to port and every movement brought a protesting scrape from under the chassis.

Dawes got down in the mud and examined the damage. 'Maybe I'll be able to fix it in the morning,' he said. His tone struck Holt as surprisingly offhand. 'No point in starting now – it'll soon be dark . . . Anyway, isn't it time to put out that booster of yours?'

Holt glanced at his watch. 'Yes, the session's on . . .' He went into the van and set up the transceiver. In a moment

Dawes joined him there. Holt spread out his notes and switched the set to 'Transmit'. As he gave Mount Henry's call sign the ether cleared as though by magic. Every outpost in the district was obviously waiting to hear the latest report from the mine. In a matter of seconds he was through to Gregory.

Gregory said: 'Go ahead, Ivor, I'm receiving you. What's the news? Over.'

'I can hardly hear you,' Holt said. 'I'm getting you at only about strength two and you keep fading. I think this set's going to pack up any minute ... The news is worse, John. The flow's increased to a hundred million gallons a day. The top pump's still working after a fashion, but it can't begin to cope. It looks as though the whole mine's going to be flooded. Over.'

A groan came from Gregory. 'God, what a disaster ... ! I tried to get up the road this afternoon, Ivor, but you were right about that bridge – it's down. We're sending a working party in first thing tomorrow with a temporary span. How's the block at your end? Over.'

'It's bigger than we thought – and the rain isn't helping. The whole place is a quagmire. We're working round the clock to clear a passage and get the phone wires joined but it could take another forty-eight hours. Tell me, are there any instructions from ...'

Holt didn't break off. He was still talking as he leaned forward and cut the current.

Dawes said, 'What's the idea?'

'That's what happens when a set suddenly conks, Frank. Now they won't expect any more messages ...' Holt gave a tired smile. 'Well, I guess that's taken care of our public relations.'

Dawes was unusually silent over supper. He seemed, Holt thought, to have more on his mind that the routine problems of the journey. After the meal was over he got out a map and studied it for a while without speaking.

'Well,' Holt said at last, 'what's the position?'

Dawes shrugged. 'Hard to tell, after all those detours . . . At a rough guess I'd say we were about five miles from the gulley we're making for. Once we're there, we'll have another three miles across the plain to the nearest point on the road, just north of Linda.'

'M'm – that doesn't sound too bad. We should be able to manage it by tomorrow night.'

'There's a chance,' Dawes agreed. 'Just a chance . . . But only if we ditch your van, Birdie.'

Holt's jaw dropped. 'Ditch the van . . . ! Why? – because of the broken spring?'

'No – because it's no bloody good in mud. It's the van that holds us up, practically every time. And tomorrow will be tougher than today . . . We'll get on twice as fast without it.'

'It's a hell of a drastic step,' Holt said. 'Don't forget we're supposed to split up when we get clear.'

'If we're lumbered with the van, we won't get clear. All we'll do is bust a gut shoving it about . . . We've got to ditch it, Birdie. It's the only way we'll get through.'

'What about the stuff in it?'

'We'll leave it. There's nothing we need except the food – and your rubber dinghy. We've finished with the transceiver . . . It's the best bet – I'm sure of that.'

Holt still looked doubtful. 'The van will be found, some time. And perhaps traced to me.'

'No . . . We'll fix it so it can't be.'

'How?'

'We'll set it alight. Burn it up. Van, papers, contents – the lot.'

There was a little silence. Then Holt said, 'Well, you're the boss now – and I guess you're right . . . It seems a pity, though – it must be worth a thousand quid.'

Dawes shook his head. 'Not to us, sport – to us it's just a bloody liability.' He grinned. 'Anyway, what's a thousand quid?'

5

Both men were out in the warm rain by first light next morning, each busy with his preparations for the fateful day ahead. Holt sorted out the things he wished to take with him, stowing his clothes, tape recorder, binoculars and stock of tinned food in the back of the Land-Rover, and lashing the deflated rubber dinghy, with its sectional oars and pump, in one large bundle on the roof rack. He also gathered up all documents that could identify the van or its purchaser – the registration book, the sales receipt, the transceiver licence – and piled them on the front seat of the Volkswagen where they would burn easily.

Dawes was occupied with a brace and bit, drilling out the van's engine and chassis numbers. When he'd finished he went over to the Land-Rover and repeated the process there. 'No harm in taking precautions,' he said, with a dour glance at the sky. Holt thought the gesture a bit theatrical, like making a will just before battle, but he didn't comment. Finally Dawes moved the Land-Rover to a safe spot, well away from the coming conflagration.

'Right,' he said, 'that's about it.' He returned to the van, splashed the contents of two petrol cans around the interior, and loosened the fuel lines. Then, standing a yard or two back, he set a light to a box of matches, tossed it through the open door, and retired briskly. There was a whoosh of flame that no rain could put out and in seconds the van was ablaze from end to end. As the heat grew more intense the main petrol tank went up with a roar, feeding the pyre. For five minutes the van and its contents burned fiercely; in ten there was little left but a smouldering ruin. Rather sombrely, Holt took his seat in the Land-Rover. The van had served him well and he would miss it. Dawes had no such sentiments. He climbed in beside Holt without a backward glance, checked his direction from the compass, and drove off.

Any reservations Holt might have had about the wisdom of ditching the Volkswagen were soon dispelled. The ground was now so soggy that even the Land-Rover bogged down from time to time – but getting it out was a simple matter compared with the struggles they'd had with the van. Usually a few branches of cut scrub under the wheels sufficed to do the trick. Only once did Dawes have to use the winch, passing the wire round the trunk of a gum tree and hauling out backwards. By midday they had oozed and ploughed their way through three miles of clay and mud, and seemed within easy striking distance of their goal.

Then the rain really started.

Holt had thought it heavy before. Now it was like that first dramatic cloudburst at the cave – an opening of the heavens. The water fell in solid, opaque masses, a thundering Niagara, crashing on the roof, obscuring the view, turning every slope into a chute and every hollow into a pool. As the two men inched their way forward, sizeable patches of ground were submerged before their eyes. Holt would have stopped and waited, but Dawes – muttering that it would get no better – kept doggedly on, doing his best to avoid the pools, keeping as far as possible to the slight elevations. Presently, though, they came to a broad gulley that had to be crossed, a red-brown stream of unknown depth. Dawes cautiously edged the Land-Rover down the bank till it stood level on the hard gulley bed with the water swirling around it. The depth appeared to be no more than eighteen inches, and the bottom reasonably flat. He opened the throttle wide to breast the current and get through in a rush. They were almost across when, close under the bank, a wheel went down in a hole and the vehicle lurched to a stop. Desperately Dawes worked his gears, trying to reverse out, trying to get some movement going again. But the wheel stayed obstinately in its hole. He looked around for a tree, a large rock, anything to haul on – but the streaming ground was bare. Not even the winch could help them now. The Land-Rover was finally and firmly stuck.

They climbed down on to the bonnet and out on to the bank, almost blinded by rain and scarcely able to breathe from the water that poured over them. The deluge, if anything, was gathering weight – and the whole watershed seemed to be emptying down this channel. Already, in the few minutes they'd been there, the level of the torrent had risen perceptibly. The floor of the Land-Rover was covered, its wheels were out of sight. Water was pounding against its side, battering at its bonnet. Suddenly it stirred in the current – and Dawes sprang into action.

'The dinghy!' he yelled above the din. 'We must have the dinghy!' He leapt back on to the bonnet and climbed to the roof. With his feet jammed against the roof rack for support, he loosed the knots around the roped-up boat. For a moment he braced himself, as the Land-Rover lurched. Then balancing precariously, he got to his feet, lifted the bundle by its rope, gave it a couple of pendulum swings, and slung it out on to the bank. He'd done it! – but not a moment too soon. The roof was rocking wildly. He dropped down on to the bonnet, steadied himself for the jump, and hurled himself at the bank. Holt grabbed him as he landed, and hauled him to safety.

In grim silence, the two men stood and watched the torrent rise, the drama move to its end. Slowly, the Land-Rover tilted as the pressure of the sideways current grew. Slowly it swung on the pivot of its fixed wheel. The bonnet disappeared, and the angle of the roof steepened. It was rolling over . . . Suddenly it freed itself from the hole – and in seconds it was swept away, carried down the steep gulley like a straw.

Now the two men had the clothes they stood up in, and the dinghy, and that was all.

Dawes shouted, above the roar of the water, 'We'll sling it between us,' and jerked his head towards the boat. Holt crooked his fingers under one end of the forty-pound roped bundle; Dawes took the other end. They didn't speak any more. The noise was deafening, there was nothing to discuss, there was only one place to go. They started to walk.

Once they'd got used to the warm bath of the rain and learned the technique of keeping their heads down in order not to drown, walking was less of a struggle than driving. Gum-booted, they could plough straight on through scrub and mud and pool that would have checked a vehicle. Occasionally one of them slipped and stumbled – but there was no bogging down. As long as they kept in step, the dinghy was no great burden. Their speed was minimal – a snail's trudge – but they were moving ... Then, as they began to think the escarpment couldn't be far ahead, they were held up by another raging stream and had to climb for a mile to find a crossing over stepping-stone rocks and descend a mile to get back on course. And all the while the rain fell down in solid sheets. As his limbs tired and his strength ebbed, Holt recalled ruefully how on his way from Darwin he'd looked forward to the modest challenge of his enterprise. No danger, he'd told himself; no hectic getaway at the end; an agreeable locale for the adventure; a playboy's dream ... ! He must have been out of his mind.

It was almost five o'clock in the afternoon when, desperately weary and very hungry, they emerged from the scrub at the fretted edge of the 'jump-up' and at last looked down upon the plain. And what a plain! Even after Dawes' warnings, even after the deluge of the day, Holt, gazing out, could scarcely believe his eyes. The land at their feet, the arid land of bleached grass and spinifex, was one great lake – a sheet of water, broken only by the tops of bushes, that seemingly stretched to infinity. Water without a horizon, water whose surface in the steely light was hardly distinguishable from the rain that poured down on it.

Thankful now that they had shed the transport which in any case would have been useless, they plunged and slithered down the rugged rocks and gulleys of the 'jump-up.' It took them nearly half an hour to reach the lakeside, so difficult were the rushing rivulets to negotiate, so awkward the roped parcel that they carried. By the time they got to the bottom the feeble glow of day was failing. 'Better pump up while we can still see,' Dawes shouted, above the rain. Holt unroped the dinghy, spread it out, loosened the valves, and applied himself to the pump. In a few minutes the boat had snaked into shape, a safe and unsinkable craft, plump and tight.

Holt gazed around. Dusk was at hand. 'Where do we make for?' he asked.

Dawes pointed. Far across the water there was a gleam of light. 'That's Linda ...'

'And what then, Frank?'

'Let's get to the road first,' Dawes said. 'Then we'll decide.' He sounded indifferent, almost resigned. No doubt he'd foreseen all this, Holt thought. He'd known what the wet would be like. He'd known that even on the bitumen, escape would be an ordeal in such weather. No wonder he'd been moody ... !

They launched the dinghy and climbed in. Dawes settled down in the stern. Holt pushed the oars through the rubber rowlocks and started to row.

There was a steady breeze heading them, and rowing against it was hard work. The water was mostly shallow, but there were currents in deeper channels that constantly swept them off their course. Every few minutes they tangled with protruding scrub and underwater grass. Myriads of insects, driven into the air by the floods, settled on every inch of bare flesh. Once they passed a knoll of higher ground, a sanctuary – judging by the strange sounds that came from it – of a whole menagerie of animals marooned by the wet. Once, among the sticks and grass and debris that floated scummily on the surface, Holt thought he saw the red eyes of a crocodile – but Dawes laughed mirthlessly, and said he was imagining things. There was still no let-up in the rain and Dawes was kept busy baling with a gumboot. From time to time Holt glanced over his shoulder, steering on the point of light.

They grounded before they came to it. The lake had ended. They pulled the boat up a streaming grass slope and then left it, feeling their way ahead. There was a gum tree, standing alone, and a gulley that ended in an arched tunnel, a culvert by the feel of it. They climbed above the culvert to a flattened causeway. They could see almost nothing in the darkness – but underfoot, for the first time in days, there was a hard, man-made surface. They had reached the bitumen at last.

Neither man had any illusions about the plight they were still in. Both were near exhaustion point from prolonged effort. They needed urgently to get away from the district; they also needed rest and food and shelter. None of these things seemed possible. Without transport and in the teeming rain they couldn't hope to get farther that night than the settlement at Linda, half a mile along the road. And when they got there they wouldn't dare to approach anyone. Contact would mean questions. Pretty searching questions, too, considering the state they were in. Where have you come from? How did you get here? What are you up to? Suspicious questions. Anyone would be suspicious of two filthy, rain-soaked, bearded figures arriving without transport at a lonely settlement on a black night in the wet...

Dawes spoke first. 'I reckon we've got one chance, Birdie.'

'I can't see one, Frank. What is it?'

'Pinch a car or a truck in Linda.'

'Linda's only a few houses,' Holt said. 'There won't be many cars about.'

'There'll be some . . . And in those outback places they often get left in the drive-in. Unlocked, too, with the keys in. It's not like a town . . . Or we might find something in one of the loading yards.'

'M'm . . . The loss would be discovered, though. It'd mean we'd have the law on our tail. What about that?'

'We could dump the car at the Curry . . . Then clean up in the public gents, sit out the night, buy a few things in the morning, and fly out before the cops got cracking.'

Holt grunted. 'What about the risk at Linda? We've only got to be seen in this state and the cops'll start checking on us . . .' His hand went to his hip pocket, where passport and papers bulged. 'They'll find our documents, check on our records. Link us with Talbot. Then everything will be down the drain.'

'Okay,' Dawes said. 'You got a better idea?'

'No, Frank, I haven't. But if we show ourselves in Linda I think the odds are we'll be picked up and questioned . . .' For a moment the silence was broken only by the drumming of the rain. Then Holt said, 'I agree we've got to risk it – it's the only chance. But I think we should look ahead – take precautions . . .'

'Like what?'

'Ditch everything that identifies us. Passports, papers – the lot.'

'But we'll need them for getting away.'

'If we manage to pinch a car,' Holt said, 'we can come back for them afterwards. If we don't, we won't have any use for them. Not for a while, anyway . . . Don't you see, if we've no papers, we can give false names, tell some story . . .'

'What story?'

'I don't know – we'll have to think of one. Couldn't we be

a couple of hoboes? I could do the Aussie accent all right – and I'm damn sure that's what we look like.'

'Yeah,' Dawes said slowly. 'Yeah – we could . . . We could say we thumbed a ride in on a truck earlier in the day. Make out we were a couple of no-hopers heading for the Gulf . . . Except we've got no swag.'

'The truck could have driven off with the swag still in it – by mistake. Who's to know?'

'That's right . . . It's an idea, Birdie – my word, yes. If we stuck to our story and kept our traps shut about everything else they couldn't even link us with the Henry.'

'And whatever happened, we'd still be able to collect our hundred thou. in the end . . . That's the line, Frank. That way we can't lose.'

'Okay,' Dawes said. 'I'm with you. Let's get to work.'

'Where'll we hide the papers?'

'We'll have to bury them – it's the only safe way . . .' Dawes peered out through the rain. The trunk of the solitary eucalypt loomed faintly against the sky. It was a good landmark – easy to find again by the lights of a car, or any time in daylight. 'I'll bury them under that tree.'

'They'll be in a fine mess by the time we need them – if things go wrong . . .'

'We'll wrap them in the dinghy's spray cover,' Dawes said. 'It's waterproof – it'll keep them like new.'

'That's an idea . . . What about the dinghy, Frank? We won't need it again – and if it's found around here it might start someone thinking.'

'You could shove it out into the water – let it blow away . . . Or stuff it into the culvert under the road.'

'Yes – that's better . . . I'll go and do it.'

'I'll come and get the cover. I need the pump, too.'

Together, they groped their way down the slope to the dinghy. Dawes unbuttoned the rubber splash cover, and collected the pump, and made his way back to the tree. There, he started to scoop out a hole in the wet ground, using the nozzle of the pump as a tool. Holt deflated the boat, and roped it up with oars inside, and carried it to the culvert.

By the time he re-joined Dawes, the hole was ready. Both men emptied their pockets – of passports, driving licences, travellers' cheques and money. All except for a couple of dollars and some loose change that Dawes kept. Even hoboes would have that. Holt wrapped everything in the splash cover and put the packet in the hole. Dawes threw the dinghy pump in on top of it, shovelled the earth back with his foot, and stamped it down.

'Right,' he said. 'I'm Bert Wilson and you're Alf Smith, and we've hitched from Sydney. A couple of Aussie bums ... Let's go.'

They plodded heavily along the streaming bitumen. They were both near the end of their strength. Holt was so tired he could barely drag one gumboot past the other. His head ached, his belly rumbled with emptiness. Food, he thought, was what they needed, even before transport. Food, and a drink of something strong, to put fresh heart in them. Food – and a few minutes of respite from this bloody rain. What a hope! What a hope of anything ... ! Still, they'd got to make this last try ... He staggered on.

They could see more lights ahead now. House lights – perhaps a dozen of them, throwing out a dangerous glow. But no street lamps – that was a relief. No proper street, apart from the bitumen. No one moving around outside – not in this weather. No cars visible. It looked as though they'd have to go on to the railway, the loading yards. Right through the settlement ...

Suddenly Dawes stopped. There was a building on the left, with no lights showing. A house on stilts, with a verandah, just discernible in silhouette against the sky. A house standing on its own, the first they'd come to. Silent – inviting ...

Dawes said: 'They often leave cars under their houses. Maybe there's one here.' He advanced cautiously into the drive. Holt followed close behind him, peering ahead through the sheet of rain. Dawes kept going. Then, abruptly, the rain was cut off. They were under cover, under the house. A respite at last. They groped around in the darkness, hands outstretched, feeling for a car. They explored every inch – but there was nothing.

Holt leaned back against one of the house supports. 'You know something, Frank? I could use some grub.'

'Me too,' Dawes said. 'My word, yes.'

'There'll be food up in the house – and there's no one there ... I reckon it's too good a chance to miss.'

'I guess you're right,' Dawes said. 'Let's take a look round.'

They groped their way back to the drive-in. The nearest building was a good hundred yards along the road. They'd be safe enough as long as they made no noise. They climbed the verandah steps and tried the front door. It was locked. They walked round the verandah to the back, trying all the windows. Behind the house they found one that was slightly open – a small one, with opaque glass. The bathroom. Dawes pushed the window up and heaved himself on to the sill and squeezed through. Holt followed him in. They had no light, not even a match, and they couldn't risk pressing a switch. They fumbled their way along a passage, entered a room. There was a smell of cooked food in the air. The kitchen! They edged round the walls, hands extended. Stove. Fridge. Dawes pulled the fridge door open and felt inside. Bottles. Milk, not beer – but more than welcome. He passed one to Holt. Now something on a dish – the remains of a chicken. Two plump legs intact. He tore the carcass apart and gave half of it to Holt. They began to eat, ravenously.

They were still eating when they heard the sound of a car. Distant at first, but approaching rapidly. The glow of headlamps showed at the window. Then, right underneath them, an engine roared and died. The owner of the house had come home. They could hear a voice. Several voices. Two men and a woman ...

'That's torn it,' Holt said softly. 'What do we do, Frank?'

Dawes was on his feet, listening. 'Hold it till they're all inside. Then nip out of the window and run like hell.'

They waited tensely, following the sounds. Footsteps on the verandah. A key turning in a lock. A drawling Queensland voice – 'How about a drink, Tom . . . ?' Dawes felt around in the darkness for the window catch. Footsteps in the passage now, approaching the kitchen. Dawes was struggling with the catch. 'The bloody thing's stuck, Birdie . . .' He gave it up and moved to the door. 'We'll have to jump them and fight our way out. Before they switch the light on.'

'I'm not much good at a punch-up,' Holt murmured.

'Don't worry, sport – I'll punch for two.'

The door opened. A feeble glow came in from the passage. A hand reached for the light switch. Dawes leapt.

For a few moments there was pandemonium – a noisy riot in the near-darkness. Dawes closed with his man, battering him with sledgehammer fists. The man fought back, slogging it out toe to toe. Somewhere in the room, Holt was struggling with the second man. A table crashed over; glass and crockery smashed. The air was thick with grunts, oaths and the thud of blows.

Dawes was holding his own – more than holding his own. He had the man pinned against the wall and was raining savage punches on his head. Any second now he'd land the knockout . . . Then someone grabbed him from behind and hauled him back. As he swung round, the pinned man recovered and hit him hard on the side of the chin. He sank groggily to the floor. There was a click, and the kitchen light went on.

He looked around in a dazed way. This first thing he saw was Holt, lying in a corner, out cold. The second thing he saw was the row of stripes on the shirt sleeve of the man whose head he'd been bashing. Three stripes of a sergeant of police . . .

He'd been bashing a cop!

*　　*　　*

As the sergeant jerked him to his feet, Dawes's overriding feeling was one of relief. Relief that they'd taken precautions . . . The immediate outlook was bleak indeed. The cooler again, for sure. Six months, he reckoned, for breaking into the house. Hoboes would get that, even if they had been looking for food. And six months for assaulting the police. You couldn't expect leniency when you'd beaten up a cop. A year for the whole job . . . But after that, back to the cache under the tree, back to England – if Talbot had done his stuff, back to a hundred thousand quid. Back to a fortune. Thanks to Birdie . . .

CHAPTER V

Talbot had indeed been doing his stuff.

On his first day in Darwin he'd spread his cover story around a little further. Since it was necessary for the plan that he should linger in the area for a day or two, he'd had to have some unfinished business to account for his delayed departure. He'd therefore visited yet another tourist office and said his well-worn piece – and he'd also made an appointment to call at the administrative headquarters of the Northern Territory on the following morning. An unmitigated bore – but necessary.

The only thing that had really interested him that day was the weather. He'd followed the forecasts with the closest attention – and he'd been happy to learn that the prognosis was still favourable. The violent thunderstorms that had been raging in the north were definitely about to give way to steadier monsoon rains. Probably in the next twenty-four hours. That meant that the timing of zero hour at the mine had been just right. Dawes and Holt would finish their job without difficulty that evening – and by the last bulletin of the day the news should be on the air.

When, at midnight, no mention was made of the Henry, Talbot knew that something had gone wrong – at least with the schedule. His imagination began to work on possible causes – a failure of Dawes' explosive to go off – a failure of Holt's transceiver to transmit – a mechanical failure in the transport – an accident ... The hold-up might only be temporary – but it was disturbing ...

He filled in part of a worrying night renewing his contact with Furneval on long-distance. He had just reached Darwin from the outback he said, after a most successful tour, and was clearing up a few residual items of business before leaving. He expected to be back in the office in two or three days. Meanwhile he'd like Furneval to put out a preliminary press release for the financial papers, which he dictated.

He slept badly, and woke in an edgy frame of mind. The radio was still silent about the Henry. At the Northern Territory HQ that morning he had the greatest difficulty in concentrating. Outside the window the rain was streaming down. Conditions at the cave must be perfect for action. The lack of news was beginning to look serious. He was back in his hotel room well before one o'clock, his transistor tuned for the next bulletin. And at one o'clock, he got what he was waiting for.

The report about the Henry was the top news item. The announcement said:

'The Mount Henry mine in North Queensland is today threatened with grave flooding as a result of a break-in of underground water. The news came shortly after eight o'clock this morning in an emergency broadcast by Mr Ivor Williams, the mine manager, following the collapse of telephone wires and part of the road linking Mount Henry with the neighbouring settlement of Linda. Mr Williams' report, which was heard by hundreds of people in the area on the Flying Doctor network, stated that water was entering the mine at the northern end of number two level at a rate of some sixty million gallons a day, and that the lower pumping station was flooded. In the manager's dramatic words, the mine was being "overwhelmed by a deluge". It is understood that no casualties have been sustained, and most of the personnel have been safely withdrawn from the mine. A further message from Mr Williams is expected by transceiver this evening.

'The following statement was issued in Melbourne this morning by Mr A. V. Richards, managing director of Mount Henry Proprietary. "All possible steps are being taken to restore communication with the mine by telephone and by road. The company's local representative at Mount Isa, Mr John Gregory, is making an immediate inspection of the reported road block. I am flying to Mount Isa with the company's Chief Engineer, Mr R. Wheeler, and the company's Chief Geological Adviser, Mr Peter Horne."

'Mr Richards declined to say anything at this stage about the possible circumstances surrounding the disaster.

'The editor of the *Mining World*, Mr Thomas Bryce, commented this morning in Melbourne: "Mount Henry has always had the reputation of being a particularly dry mine, and the presence of a large underground water pocket was never suspected. The mines's two pumps were installed to deal with ordinary seepage, not with an inflow approaching the reported rate, and unless the reservoir quickly empties it is difficult to see how the mine can be saved. A break-in of such proportions in this area comes as a major shock to the mining industry, and at present experts are at a loss to explain it".'

Talbot spent the whole of the afternoon beside his radio. Several times the programme was interrupted for the latest news flashes – including a report that Gregory's first attempt to reach the road block had been frustrated by a collapsed bridge. Talbot found that very heartening. After the initial delay, everything had obviously gone according to plan.

He continued to listen – and in the early evening came the item he'd been most eager to hear. It followed a recapitulation of the disaster story, and it said: 'There has been very heavy selling of the widely-held Mount Henry shares on all Australian stock exchanges throughout the day. The ordinary shares, which yesterday stood at 8 dollars, had fallen by the close of business to 4.5 dollars with no buyers in sight. Something like 40 million dollars has been wiped off the capital valuation of Mount Henry in the course of a single day. In view of the absence of hopeful news, dealers expect the spate of selling to be resumed immediately markets re-open.'

Finally, in a bulletin at ten o'clock, there came a second announcement from the mine. 'Mr Ivor Williams, the manager at Mount Henry, reported this evening by transceiver that the flow of water into the mine has increased to a rate of a hundred million gallons a day. "It looks," he said, "as though the whole mine is going to fill." Shortly afterwards Mr Williams was cut off in mid-sentence, and it is believed that the transceiver he was using has failed . . .'

Talbot gave a long sigh of satisfaction, and switched off his set. Dawes and Holt had obviously executed their tasks with flawless precision – even to the booster. Now it was up to him. He rang through to the hotel switchboard and arranged for a personal call to Prendergast for eleven PM Darwin time, which would be shortly after the start of business on the London Stock Exchange.

The call came through at eleven-ten. Talbot walked slowly to the telephone, drew a long breath, and lifted the receiver for the most important conversation of his life. In a moment he heard the familiar voice of the broker – clear, friendly, relaxed. 'Hallo, Mr Talbot. How are you?'

'Fine,' Talbot said. 'I've had a grand trip – now I'm just clearing up a few things here before flying home . . . Tell me, what's the feeling in London about this Mount Henry affair?'

'Numbed, Mr Talbot. It's the sensation of the day, of course. What a disaster!'

'How are the shares standing at the moment?'

'They're not standing at all – they're toppling. The crack here is that the jobbers are quoting high and low tides, not prices . . . ! Hold on a second – I'll look at the tape . . .' There was a short pause. 'Thirty-five shillings was the last marking we've got. That's well under half the price before the news broke.'

'Are there any cheap buyers about?'

'None at all, so far – everybody's unloading after Williams' second report. They're saying here it could take up to two years to de-water the mine and get it back to full production ... Why, are you interested?

'Yes,' Talbot said. 'I'd like you to start buying right away for my personal account. I'll pay thirty-five shillings or less – and I want the purchase completed today, before the market has time for second thoughts. I propose to invest three hundred thousand pounds.'

A low whistle came through the receiver. 'Do you really think that's wise, Mr Talbot? The experts here are talking the shares down to thirty shillings, and recovery will be very slow ... It's your affair, of course, but I'm sure you remember that your last mining venture came really unstuck.'

'It came unstuck because I believed the first reports,' Talbot said. 'They turned out to be greatly exaggerated, and if I'd held on I'd have been okay ... I may be in a tiny minority over Mount Henry, but I have a hunch this panic is being overdone too. I ran into an engineer this morning who knows the mine well, and he says there just isn't that much water around in the local rocks. He says the reservoir must be a small one, and that it'll dry up before the mine's flooded. He impressed me a lot, and I feel like backing his judgment.'

Prendergast grunted. 'Well, you could be right, I suppose – I saw a quote from the Australian *Mining World* this morning that rather tended in the same direction ... Personally I wouldn't touch it, but if you feel like a gamble it's your pigeon ... Right, I'll start buying.'

'How much do you think the price will rise against us?'

'The way things are at the moment, not a lot. The selling's a flood – I'd guess your three hundred thousand will be less than a thumb in the dyke. And I may be able to buy a block at a special price. I'll be as discreet as I can – don't worry.'

'Fine,' Talbot said. 'Now would you do me a favour, and ring me from your home after hours – say around eight o'clock your time – and confirm that the deals are through, and tell me the price?'

'I'll do that with pleasure, Mr Talbot. Where do I ring you?'

Talbot gave him the hotel number. 'And thanks a lot, Harry ... I'll look forward to hearing from you.'

He hung up, and went and mixed himself a stiff drink.

Once more, he slept uneasily. Success seemed no longer in doubt – but he couldn't be sure till he had that confirmation. He woke early, ordered strong coffee, watched the rain through the window, padded restlessly about the suite, waiting for the phone to ring. He was shaving when, at eight in the morning Darwin time, the call came through.

He snatched the receiver. 'Talbot here.'

'Prendergast ... Here's the report, Mr Talbot. You now own 182,000 ordinary shares in Mount Henry and they've cost you an average price of thirty-three shillings each ... I hope that's satisfactory.'

'Yes, Harry, that's fine – and I'm much obliged to you for ringing. I'll look in when I get back, and have a chat ... Anything else?'

Prendergast chuckled. 'Only that I wish you luck, sir! Goodbye.'

Talbot sat smiling on his bed, making the most enjoyable mental calculations of his entire career.

In a few days' time, when the true position at the Henry became known and the flap was over, the shares would rapidly return to their former value. What he had just bought for thirty-three shillings apiece, he would sell for around seventy-four shillings. At a profit of forty-one shillings a share for 182,000 shares he would clear over £370,000. Less £200,000 for Dawes and Holt. £170,000 of lovely, liquid lolly!

Now he had nothing more to worry about. He could clear his unrevealed debt to the Corporation's depositors with ease. His future was safe and bright. Tycoonery was still his to command.

He had no fears about any inquiries. There would, of course, be a tremendous inquest into the whole Henry affair and it would quickly become known that the 'disaster' had been staged. It would be discovered, too, that he – and perhaps only he – had made a packet out of it. But nobody would be able to pin anything on him. He hadn't been seen near the mine. Neither had Dawes nor Holt. Nothing could emerge to throw suspicion on any of them. And his cover story would stand up to any examination.

In all probability his good fortune would be put down to exceptional astuteness. He'd be the man who'd learned the lesson of a past investment failure, who'd listened this time to the advice of people with local experience, who'd refused to believe that bad news was ever quite as bad as it seemed at first. He'd be held up as a model in the City, an optimist with flair. His already high reputation would be enhanced. Talbot the whizz-kid . . .

There was no free seat on a London-bound plane that day, but he managed to make a reservation for the following morning. In any other circumstances a day to kill in Darwin – out of season, and with the monsoon rains sweeping in unbroken from the sea – would have seemed a pretty unattractive prospect. But to Talbot it was a glorious day, bright with interior sunshine. He lingered contentedly over the morning papers, enjoying in a detached way a long account of the efforts being made to clear the two blocks on the road to the Henry. He listened with interest to a report at midday that the fallen bridge had been replaced. He spent a good deal of time in the hotel bar, chatting to people for whom the disaster at the Henry was the only possible topic. Many of them had lost money, and he duly sympathized. In the afternoon he caught up on his sleep; in the evening he dined well. His night's rest was undisturbed by anxiety or dream. Early next morning, refreshed and supremely cheerful, he took a taxi to the airport. Thirty-six hours later he was in London.

As he passed a bookstall on his way out of Heathrow his glance fell on a copy of that morning's *Financial Times*, tightly folded in a rack. Its headline, in large type across four columns, was MT. HENRY MINE FLOODED. Talbot was a little surprised that the true facts hadn't yet come out – obviously it was taking longer than he'd expected to re-open communications with the mine. He bought the paper and turned to the share price pages, interested to see if the Henry shares had fallen any further since his purchase. H'm – thirty-one shillings. If he'd waited a bit longer he'd have made an extra twenty thou. But if he'd waited too long he might have missed the boat altogether. He hadn't any complaints. He folded the paper and stuffed it in his pocket.

It was just after eight in the evening when he reached his Mayfair flat. The long flight across the world had had the usual effect on him – a slight sense of disembodiment and a total loss of appetite. He would skip dinner, he decided, and have an early night. He went into the kitchen, poured himself a Scotch-on-the-rocks, collected the *Financial Times* from his overcoat pocket, and dropped into a chair.

He opened the paper – and stared aghast at what he saw. In an instant, promise and fulfilment were shattered. The fools . . . ! After all his thought and care, all the planning and effort, Dawes and Holt had bungled it . . .

What he'd read at the airport was only part of the headline – the first four words. The rest had been folded over. The full headline was: MT. HENRY MINE FLOODED BY DIVERTED

RIVER. Below was a line in smaller type: REPORTS OF UNDERGROUND BREAK-IN DENIED. And below that again, the sickening story...

'The Mount Henry Mine is flooded – but not, as was first reported, by a break-in of underground water. An official announcement issued in Melbourne last night stated that violent monsoon rains, sweeping down the narrow valley below the mine, had been damned up by a huge fall of rock and mullock that had completely blocked the exit. The swollen river, unable to follow its usual channel, had become diverted into an old working of the mine and thence into the main shaft. The pumps had been unable to cope with the rush of water, and the mine had filled.

'The remarkable series of events that brought about this disaster are now being investigated by the Queensland police. All the facts seem to point to a criminal conspiracy that went wrong.

'Following the restoration of telephone communications between the mine and Mount Isa yesterday, it was learned that recent reports of an underground break-in purporting to come from the mine manager, Mr Ivor Williams on the mine's emergency radio transmitter, had not in fact emanated from him or from anyone else at Mount Henry, and were totally false. It has also been established that a road bridge, thought at first to have collapsed through stress of weather, was blown up by explosive. The fall which blocked the road near the mine and caused the eventual inundation is now also believed to have been the result of an explosion. These facts, together with the discovery that the transceiver at Mount Henry had been tampered with and rendered unserviceable, all point to the deliberate isolation of the mine by persons unknown.

'The possibility that the affair was intended as no more than a gigantic hoax by a group of ill-disposed men is generally scouted, in view of the tremendous effort and organization involved. Police are working on the theory – which would seem to be the only rational explanation of the conspiracy – that the criminals aimed to bring about a catastrophic fall in the company's shares by spreading false reports of a flood, and then to buy at panic prices for a recovery. On this theory, the diversion of the river would have been an unforeseen and accidental development, wrecking the conspirators' plans as well as the mine . . .'

Talbot laid the paper aside, and sat motionless. He could picture the scene only too well – the huge tip coming down and choking the bottle-neck of the valley; the watercourse still dry enough at the time to be no obvious menace; Dawes and Holt overlooking the danger in their eagerness to get away and finish the job . . . And then, once the monsoon had started, a raging flood pouring into the cave and down the tunnel, sweeping aside whatever was left of the ancient wooden gate . . .

So the brilliant plan had come to nothing. And now, Talbot saw with fearful clarity, his position was worse than if the plan had never been conceived. Not only had he failed to make the profit he needed to replace the funds of the Corporation's depositors – he couldn't even sell the shares he'd bought for what he'd contracted to pay for them. He was more hopelessly in the red than ever – and if he stayed in London, he was finished. The gates of Wormwood Scrubs were creaking open for him. It had come at last – the stark alternative. Flight . . .

Coolly, but quickly, he made his dispositions. If he was going, the time to go was now, before the hounds got on his trail. And Brazil was the place – he'd decided that long ago. He'd be welcomed at first as a well-to-do tourist. Afterwards he could lose himself there, take a new name, make a new life. He was young enough, and he still had his wits. He reached for the phone and called London Airport. Yes, there was a flight leaving for Rio that evening – but he must be at the airport within an hour. He made the reservation and repacked his case. Passport and money – they were the main things. From the safe behind the picture he took the great wad of US dollars that he'd kept against contingencies. Too big for a pocket – they'd have to go in the case. A tiny risk – but in all his journeys he'd never had a case opened on his way out of the country. Anyway, the risk had to be taken ...

He glanced at his watch. With time so short, he'd barely make it in a taxi. He left the flat and went down quickly to the lock-up garage where he kept the Aston. It was months since he'd used the car – but it had been serviced regularly and should be in good order. In fact the engine started at the first touch of the button. In seconds he was on his way.

The traffic, as always, was heavy, and he had bad luck with the lights. Red all the way, it seemed. As the minutes rushed by, he began to get seriously worried about missing the plane. Between lights he gave the Aston all it had, thinking only of escape and the haven of Brazil. Then a black car swept by, pulled across in front of him, and rang him to halt. He had barely time for a curse, let alone a thought, before two policemen were walking stolidly towards him. One was a sergeant.

'Good evening, sir,' the sergeant said. 'Are you aware that you were doing seventy miles an hour in a built-up area?'

'Was I really? I'm sorry, Sergeant – I didn't realize ... I'm trying to catch a plane.'

'I'm afraid that's no excuse, sir. This is not a racing track, this is a public highway ... May I see your licence?'

Automatically, Talbot flicked open the glove compartment. It was only as his hand closed on the licence that he remembered – and by then it was too late. The sergeant was reaching for it. Talbot sat as though paralysed. For the first time in his life, he could think of absolutely no way out.

'Disqualified, eh?' The sergeant's tone was suddenly sharp.

He peered into the back of the car. 'Where are you making for?'

'Brazil,' Talbot said. 'On business. I'm the chairman of the Commonwealth Loan Corporation, and it's vital I get there tomorrow . . . A big export order,' he added hopefully.

'You'll be lucky,' the sergeant said. 'Driving while disqualified is a very serious offence.'

'I know it is, Sergeant – I'm afraid I forgot about it because of the urgency. Can't I answer your summons when I get back? I admit the offence – I'll plead guilty.'

'Not a hope,' the sergeant said. 'Do you mind opening that case?'

'Do I have to?'

'If you don't open it here, you'll open it at the station.'

'I see . . .' Talbot reached for the case, pressed the catch and pushed back the lid. The sergeant fumbled among the clothes and papers – and pulled out the wad of dollars.

'Right, my lad,' he said. 'You'd better come along with us.'

Talbot sat back in the police car with the sergeant beside him. Already, he'd begun to reconcile himself to the inevitable. It was going to be hell, back in the Scrubs, for seven years, or five years, or whatever. No question about that . . . But at least he'd had fun on the way. It had been a whale of a plot he'd dreamed up – a plot that deserved to go down in history. He'd gambled and lost – but he'd almost won. And he certainly wasn't going to whine because the law had caught up with him. He still reckoned himself a good loser – and after all, he'd asked for it . . .

Phrases came into his mind – and suddenly he chuckled.

'What's so funny?' the sergeant asked.

Talbot turned to him, smiling in the darkness. 'Just a private joke, Sergeant . . . I don't suppose you ever heard of a man called Horatio Bottomley.'

Andrew Garve

'Is without rival in the business of dreaming up original ideas about which to write excellent crime stories' – THE BIRMINGHAM POST

FRAME-UP 25p

THE FAR SANDS 25p
'Grade A thriller' – SUNDAY TELEGRAPH

THE HOUSE OF SOLDIERS 25p
'Brilliant' – BOSTON GLOBE

THE ASHES OF LODA 25p
'Hairbreadth escapes' – NEW YORK TIMES

'It is impossible for Andrew Garve to be anything but superbly readable' – GUARDIAN

These and other PAN Books are obtainable from all booksellers and newsagents. If you have any difficulty please send purchase price plus 7p postage to PO Box 11, Falmouth, Cornwall.
While every effort is made to keep prices low, it is sometimes necessary to increase prices at short notice. PAN Books reserve the right to show new retail prices on covers which may differ from those advertised in the text or elsewhere.